REMAKING THE SORCERESS

NATALIE BARTLEY

TEA WITH COFFEE MEDIA

Remaking the Sorceress, Copyright © 2022, by Natalie Bartley.

Cover and Internal Design © 2022 by Tea With Coffee Media

Cover Design by Victoria Moxely/Tea With Coffee Media

Cover Images by Dreamstime

Internal Images © Kelsey Anne Lovelady via Canva

Tea With Coffee Media and the colophon are trademarks of Tea With Coffee Media

Published by Tea With Coffee Media

teawithcoffee.media

Cataloging-in-Publication Data is on file with the Library of Congress.

Print ISBN#—978-1-957893-11-2

Ebook ISBN#— 978-1-957893-16-7

Bowmanville, Ontario, Canada

Published by Tea With Coffee Media

This story involves coarse language, sexual situations, violence, and scenes that may not be appropriate for all readers. Reader discretion is advised.

All similarities to other works are entirely coincidental.

I dedicate *Remaking the Sorceress* to my fiancé, Brian; without whose support, I would never have finished this story. I also dedicate this to the old crew with the Legends of the Veil blog, where my Medea was born. I originally meant for this story (most of it) to be her next arc, but life got in the way, and I needed to leave the project. So here is my ode to them. Thank you, all of you, for sticking by me while Medea screamed at me incessantly.

Thank you to my first editor, Sean Sweeney, for keeping me on track and getting this story completed, and for helping to teach me to show not tell.

CONTENTS

"As for Medea,

    that poor lady, in her disgrace, cries out,

    repeating his oaths, recalling the great trust

    in that right hand with which he pledged his love.

    She keeps calling to the gods to witness

    how Jason is repaying her favours.

    She just lies there. She won't eat—her body

    she surrenders to the pain, wasting away,

    always in tears, ever since she found out

    how her husband has dishonoured her.

    She's not lifted her eyes up from the ground,

    or raised her head. She listens to advice,

    even from friends, as if she were a stone,

    or the ocean swell, except now and then

    she twists that white neck of hers and weeps,

    crying to herself for her dear father, her home,

    her own land, all those things she left behind,

    to come here with the man who now discards her."

lines 26-43 from *Medea* by Euripides

    (Translated by Ian Johnston Vancouver Island University Nanaimo,

British Columbia Canada ian.johnston@viu.ca, First Published 2008, Revised 2015)

I

THE QUEST BEGINS

In all the millennia that I had walked along this primitive world, I had never felt this frozen before. It was a cold which felt like I had taken a dip in the Arctic Ocean and had been held in by unseen hands for far too long. Even the flames of the sun could not warm me.

But I suppose that's what happens when your magic, fire, and life source suddenly abandon you.

I should back up and tell you who I am. My name is Medea—yes, *that* Medea; no, there's no need to hide your children. Not any longer. I was wife to Jason, that scoundrel, and daughter of the half-Titan Aeëtes and of Idyia, the Oceanid, granddaughter to mighty Helios and Perseis; at one time they dubbed me the Sorceress of Colchis, Mistress of Potions, Protector of the Golden Fleece—and even that is a misnomer, given that I stole the damn thing—you *should* know them all by now. Hell, I might have forgotten a few that Elizabeth the First bestowed on me when we, shall we say, dabbled in the Tower. And yes ... I did all those horrible things of which I am accused.

It is also true, that the Furies hounded me for centuries for one particular crime before stopping and inexplicably giving up. I'm not sure *why* they ended their chase, but I was glad for it. But that is a story for another day. This is the story of how I regained my powers, rekindled the fire within, and grew to be one of the most powerful sorceresses in the modern world.

On the day in question, I took a walk down the beach near my apothecary. It was the usual thing I did when business went slower than slumber; thanks to the ocean and sun flowing through my veins, I always felt more at home near the water, whether it be a pond, river, stream, or the sea. Yet as I passed the Point, I felt weakened somehow. I couldn't explain it. A rush of sub-Arctic air suddenly permeated my flesh and hit me in my gut; my eyes widened at the sudden intrusion. And while I struggled to remain upright, my knees eventually hit the cold sand.

Heartbeats later, Kide, my dragon—a gigantic beast of massive scale, complete with rock-hard, blue-black hide, with eyes of the darkest obsidian—and my lifelong, soul-bound partner and purveyor of our crimes, emerged by my side in his human form, the telltale pop hitting my ears and drowning out the rage of my rushing headache for a few seconds. My aunt Kirke, such a dear, wizened witch, had taught me a spell she had used to change men into animals and back just before my thirteenth name day, and many years later, I gave it to Kide to use at his will.

Usually, we were one person, body and soul. But now, in my searing, freezing pain, Kide knelt beside me as I shook, shivering uncontrollably. My teeth felt like they would shatter if I couldn't stop chattering!

"Shh, Medea, it's alright." Kide wrapped me in his arms and held me, warming me with comforting strokes and his own internal fire. Still, it was not enough to make me feel whole. I buried my face in his arm, feeling like an infant in need of her parents.

"What's going on, Kide? I feel weak." The words felt caustic in my throat, coming out as more of a whisper than a spoken word.

I watched as he passed a hand over my back and felt his magic coursing through me, but not reacting with my own. He confirmed my fears; his voice came through soft, yet it felt like a knife cutting into my soul.

"Your magic, Medea, has left you."

I closed my eyes and shuddered. My magic, especially the gift of sun-fire, the gift from Helios, had vanished. I was no longer immortal; no longer *whole*.

"I knew it, somehow. It was like the breath left my body, only to be replaced with stale air. I'm barely breathing." My eyes met Kide's, and while he saw my fear as clear as day, I saw watery concern staring back at me. "Why, though, what did I do? Recently, that is. The gods can't be punishing me now for my boys. That was over three thousand years ago."

Kide picked me up and cradled me in his arms as he made his way back to the small hut we used as our house.

I never needed much. I grew out of the glamour and limelight when I went into "hiding". Even when I went into town and mingled with the mortals, I chose a different name. 'Medea' still evoked a sense of fear and hatred. I think it has been ingrained into humanity since my exile from the Mediterranean. I could return, but nothing there would be familiar to me any longer, and I felt no connection to the land I once called home.

When we entered the house, my breath hung before me in icy crystals; goose flesh dotted my forearms, and the chattering teeth were still there, though not as prevalent as before. I had never noticed the cold before because my inner fire always kept me warm. But now, in the middle of summer, I froze. Another shiver swept through me, and Kide sparked a fire in the hearth before placing me on the couch. I pulled out my phone and dialed the only other witch I knew that may have faced something like this before.

The line rang twice before a heavily stilted Russian accent roared through.

"Hello, Medea, vy are you calling me at this ungodly hour?"

I easily detected the agitation in Baba Yaga's voice. Then again, Baba Yaga seemed to have agitation engrained in her DNA. It was certainly written on her business cards.

"Baba, I'm sorry. I need your help." I paused. I never asked for help, especially not from her. She was older than me, wiser than me, and fucking scarier than me.

"Vhat do you need, my child?"

I cringed. I was not too fond of being called a child, but I was one, compared to her.

"I ..." I froze. How do you tell the Witch of Russia that you've lost your powers?

"Out vith it Medea, I grow old vaiting for you."

I sputtered out the words quickly. She could cast compulsion through the phone, and I was in no shape to stop her. "I have no magic; it's all gone."

I heard a clunk and some swearing in Russian, and then, "vhat do you mean, you have no powers? Vhere did they go?"

I frowned. The worry in her voice made my chest deflate.

"I don't know, that's... that's why I need your help. They just abandoned me."

"It was sudden, Baba, no warning, nothing," Kide piped in.

"Is that your dragon? He's a fine-looking man. I have missed him." I saw a blush rise to Kide's cheek, and I chuckled. "Do you still have the mirror I gave you?"

I looked over at Kide, who turned and hurried to our storage locker. He rummaged through and pulled it out.

"Yes, why?"

Baba sighed. "You need to contact the other side. Only they can tell you what you need to know."

I stared at the mirror. I was not particularly eager to use it because it reminded me of my pain, my past, and most of all, my failures.

"Why, Baba? Why this way?" I sounded small and timid, and I was. It terrified me to use this mirror, to take this path. I hadn't felt this frightened in nearly three thousand years.

"If I had the answer to that, Medea, I still vouldn't tell you. It would be best if you learned this for yourself. I know it vill be hard, and you can lean on me venever you need, dear." Hearing her voice, caring and worried, almost had me in tears. Baba helped me a lot after I fled Greece, more so than I had ever admitted.

"Thank you, Baba. I hope I won't need your help, but with me, you never know. Umm, please don't tell anyone else. You know what would happen if the others found out." I shuddered at the thought of the other witches and sorceresses around the world, finding out that I was mortal again. I mean, I could probably die right now, and then I'd be Tartarus-bound.

"When those who 'love' you see you as weak, you leave. There are no ifs, ands, or buts about it. That's what the Americans say. Surround yourself with those who will lift you out of love and caring, not out of pity and disrespect," Kide added before Baba Yaga had the chance to speak. "If the rest of the community can't appreciate the predicament that you're in, then to Hell with them."

I looked over at my dearest friend. It was rare for him to be outspoken like this.

"I agree vith the dragon-man, ve are few and far between, us powerful vitches. Ve need to stick together. Use the mirror, Medea, and call me if you need more help." With that, Baba Yaga hung up, and silence lingered.

I set my phone down and looked over at Kide. "I can't use the mirror, though. Not without my power."

"I can activate it, but you need to stand in front of it so that it will show you your path," he said as he passed me the mirror.

"Now? We're doing this now?" I looked at him, the terror welling. I had just gone through a life-altering experience, and the dratted dragon wanted me to simply pick up and continue as if nothing had happened? Besides, the images I'd seen in this mirror were never pretty, never good.

"Why not? Do you want to remain this way for the rest of your life? However long that will be?"

I stared at him, hard, then turned back to the mirror.

"Do it, Kide, but stay with me, please," I replied. Kide sat down beside me, held my hand, and activated the mirror with a sweeping wave.

I closed my eyes and focused on regaining my powers on the path I would need to take. "Mater!" I heard the voices of two young boys ring out, and my heart skipped a beat. Why them? When I opened my eyes, I smiled brightly at them.

"Mermerus, Pheres!" I cried out, glad and horrified all at the same time to see my sons, my precious sons, these two beautiful children that I had murdered out of hatred and jealousy, appearing before me from the Elysian Fields. I could never, would never, wipe their blood from my hands. For this crime, the gods—my ancestors—bound me for Tartarus, and I made peace with that millennia ago. Ever since the Furies stopped chasing me for my infanticide, I still felt tremors in the tiniest space in my mind; they still haunted my steps, and Kide, bless him, always tried to reassure me they no longer gave chase. "Why, you two?"

"Because we thought you'd need a friendly face." They always spoke as one, Mermerus' voice a little deeper than Pheres, although they were both still children when they died at my hand. Friendly, though... they do realize I murdered them, right?

"Did you... did you know this was coming?" My face must have blanched because I felt Kide's hand on my back, soothing me.

"We're sorry, Mater. We have known since we died." I choked. "We couldn't tell you, not until it happened. It's like..." they looked at each other, "it's like our voices were frozen. But now we can tell you about your journey."

"My journey?" I was too stunned to ask further or to dig deeper.

My boys nodded, their faces swirling, almost like a yin and yang in the glass. It meant we had little time left before their essences faded to nothing. "Yes, you will need to travel to find the people you have wronged or failed in the past and make amends. You have walked the line between good and evil for too long, Mater. You need to settle on a path, to focus yourself on the light, or your strength will never return, and you will never see us in the afterlife."

"I never expected to see you when I died. I need to pay for my crimes." I caught sight of my face in the mirror, mixed in with my boys, and noticed the tears streaking down my face. My tears felt like rolling icicles. "The light, is it possible?"

"It is. You need to redeem our family honour. Helios was the titan of light, but he was not an evil being. His children, Aeëtes and Kirke, tarnished his name. Pasiphaë attempted to be better than her older siblings, but the gods cursed her and she suffered for it like you. It would be best if you broke the cycle. You have been stuck in time, never moving forward, ever since you left Greece, ever since us. And we do not blame you, Mater."

I started sobbing, clutching my knees to my chest. "But you cannot see that, to gain our forgiveness until the end of your journey. We are your beginning and your end."

I looked up at them, my beautiful boys, and for a moment saw their father in them, but felt no hatred there. "I'll make it to you, I promise. Where do I go first?"

They looked at each other and smiled. "To a lost love." I raised my eyebrow and looked over at Kide, who shrugged his shoulders. "The land commonly referred to as Transylvania. You need to make amends with Dracula."

My back stiffened, and even Kide paled. "That's my first task? The impossible?"

"It isn't impossible. I'm sure you have nothing to fear, Mater."

"I'm a mortal, strolling into the lair of one of the most notable and most feared vampires in the world! And I have to do it alone."

To the side, I caught Kide bowing his head in shame.

"Alone, Mater?" They asked, voices fading even more.

"Yes, alone. Kide... Kide cannot enter the castle proper, which was my fault. I cursed him, and I shouldn't have."

"Oh, well, he can get you close, and then you'll have to go in on your own. We have faith in you, Mater, we believe in you." Their voices disappeared, and I watched as their faces faded from the mirror.

Once the mirror went dark, I curled up on the couch in Kide's arms and let my grief tumble through me. He said nothing, my dearest friend, and for that, I was grateful. This journey, this trial, had barely begun, and already I felt broken by it. I didn't know how I would make it through this next section, not without Kide, not so soon. Kide just wrapped his arms around me and let me sob. We'd plan the trip from Washington to Transylvania later, but for now, I just needed to absorb everything and let it all out.

II
VLAD DRACUL ISN'T
WHERE HE'S
SUPPOSED TO BE

Kide and I spent the next few days packing and getting ready for our trip. I didn't enjoy the fact that I'd be going in on my own, but I also didn't want Kide to see me making a fool of myself if I needed to grovel. I remembered everything like it was second nature: the layout, the numerous halls to explore, the pleasure of every night spent there until the end when it all went to Tartarus in a *pithos*. Looking around our tiny house, I sighed. I had a feeling that I wouldn't be back here for a long time. I slung the pack over my shoulder with a few changes of clothing in it and took Kide's proffered hand.

"Are you ready?" he asked softly. I saw in his watery, sad eyes that he knew how hard this would be for me, and with this first step being done on my own, I knew that he felt terrible for the reasons behind it.

"I am. I'm just surprised that the curse is still intact, given the time and now lack of power there is to back it," I chuckled as he wrapped his arms around me.

"You know that isn't how curses work. You put effort and emotion into it; it wasn't going to simply disappear."

I sighed and nodded before the air rushed out of my lungs and we entered the piercing black of the void. Translocation wasn't my favourite way to travel. In the second it took to cross continents, my hair blew out in tousled waves around us, blinding me as we exited the black space.

I braced myself against the cool air as we emerged, and as soon as I had my footing about me, I looked around. The small village near the castle had grown into a bustling town, but I still couldn't remember its name; it had been a few centuries since I had last been here. We had planned to stop in at a local café before splitting up, quite possibly for the last time. As we sat down, with coffee on the way, Kide picked up a newspaper and began filtering through it.

"Shit, Medea." He held the paper out, and I looked at it.

"A wealthy Romanian socialite who bought the film rights to a popular book series has been identified as our very own Vlad Dracul. Dracul has come from a long line of Dracul's and has recently made the move to Hollywood in a drastic change from the lives of his predecessors."

"Are you fucking kidding me? We went in the wrong direction!" Out of the corner of my eye, I see a few of the nearest patrons swivel their heads, intent on finding the source of the outburst. Their conversations died, but the atmospheric music in the cafe didn't. My neck seemingly turned to gelatin as my head tumbled toward the table. The waitress approached with apprehensive steps, our coffees on a platter. She set them down and retreated behind the counter in half the time it took Kide and I to Translocate.

"So, we head back to the U.S. and over to Hollywood. It's not a big deal, Medea," he said, his tone gentle and soothing.

I lifted my head up slowly and sipped the coffee while nodding. I had caught his tone and knew why he had spoken in such reasonable, measured tones: he didn't want to offend or upset me, knowing that we had come all this way for practically nothing. I honestly didn't know why he looked so, shall we say, *scared* of me; it's not like I had the magical abilities to turn him into a newt, or dispose of him like I did with my own flesh and blood. "Oh, this is good. Let's just enjoy this before we leave."

Kide nodded and drank his coffee as well. We enjoyed the peace and tranquility of our coffee before paying and heading back out into the street. Kide found a quiet alley, and we translocated once more to the noisiest city I'd ever been in.

"How are we going to find him now?" I asked. "Los Angeles is massive."

Kide took a deep breath, and I watched as his eyes shifted into a deep, dark red. He'd caught Drac's scent. My dragon wrapped me in his arms once more, and we tore through the sky. Tiny water droplets tickled my already chilled skin, and I shook in Kide's arms before he dropped us suddenly in front of a beautiful wrought-iron gate. "This is it. I can go no further. The curse traveled with him."

I sighed. I realized I had gotten my hopes up when we discovered that Drac had moved, thinking that the curse would remain with the original place, not the host.

"I understand. Now get going. Find a place to stay, and I'll let you know when I'm ready to leave."

Kide nodded, kissed my forehead, and then took off with a powerful shove from his thighs. I watched him until he faded to nothingness.

I took a deep breath before leaving the gate and walking the perimeter of the fence, trying to find a way in. The good thing was, not all of my skills were tied to my magic. I retained my abilities as an expert hunter and tracker, having survived in the forests for years. Once I found a weak point, it didn't take long before I was over the imposing fence, my feet landing as soft as a cat – the stress on my knee tendons was a different story – and finding my way back to the door. As I neared it, I realized just how large the house was and how expansive the grounds were here; it would be easy to lose someone. Drac's palace in Transylvania was slightly smaller, if not as grandiose.

"Hollywood," I muttered, then bit the accompanying curse off before I let it slip. I looked for guards, other vamps who might give me cause for concern, and for the first time since Kide and I translocated, I felt trepidation surge into my mind, but not only that, I felt the panicked sensation of claustrophobia, of Vlad's henchmen chaining me to a wall, helpless, unable to tear myself away. My feet tried to take me in the opposite direction, away from Drac and the reckoning I faced, but I remembered my boys' faces and steeled myself.

With every ounce of my courage, I walked up to the door and pounded my fist against the oak as hard as possible until my flesh and bones ached.

The door swung open, my old flame doing the honors.

"How do you people keep getting in here? I specifically-" Drac yelled, stopping short as soon as he saw me. If he had any blood in his face, it would have rushed away and left him a bleak, sweating mess. His handsome face, though, sunk in a mix of disappointment, surprise, and fear. I tried smiling, but I just froze. "Oh, you. What are you doing here?"

I shrugged.

"Oh, you know, I was in the area..."

Yup, I thought. Just a social call. I would have telephoned ahead, but, you know, you moved and shit, didn't leave a forwarding address, didn't text, did nothing. Nada! Then again, why would you? I walked out on you, on us...

"Just in the area?! Bah!" Dracula said, his usual fed up gesture apparent as he slid behind the door and reluctantly let me in. I tried to keep my nerves and heartbeat steady, but that task grew slightly more difficult with each passing minute. "You smell different..." he drew the word out as if trying to figure out what he was sensing while he spoke. "But seriously, Medea, why are you here?"

"I need your help." There, I said it. Gods, the words burned in my throat, but the look on Drac's face nearly had me running for the door. Instead, the door slammed shut on its own, and I just looked up at my old friend.

"*You* need *my* help?" Dracula burst out laughing, devolving into cackles before he spoke again. "You broke my heart five-hundred years ago, and now you need *my* help?" He just kept laughing as we walked through the mansion, and I followed, half a trepidatious step behind. I had to admit its size left a massive impression on me; compared to the hovel in which I now – had? – resided, I could have easily gotten lost without Vlad guiding me. To be fair, I would have gotten lost in the stable.

The wood paneling reminded me of those old Tudor-style homes, and where I would have expected torches and candelabras flickering and sending the shadows running, I found golden light fixtures with steady lights. It was certainly an upgrade to the last place he had, and I was impressed with the beauty. The house had some classic charms, of course, and he had brought a few of his old-world pieces here. The house was half-museum, half-mausoleum. But that's just how the Dracul's rolled anyway.

"The house, it's gorgeous," I muttered softly as I trailed behind the vampire.

"Yes, I'm quite proud of it." Drac's voice got serious for a moment, and then he burst out laughing again.

"I don't know what's so funny, young man. It's not like I've never needed your help before," I huffed slightly as Dracula opened the door to the library. My eyes bulged at the sight. Hundreds, if not thousands of tomes, some older than dust and some newly published, the spines unbroken, rested upon solid oak shelves, from floor to ceiling. I just walked in and stared, forgetting for a while why I was there. I don't know how long I walked the room, admiring Dracula's collection before he coughed, bringing me back to myself and the problem at hand.

"What do you need from me, Medea of Colchis? I don't think you came all this way to admire my collection."

"No, but if I had known you have Salvatore and Dalglish and Sweeney and Simpson, I'd have come sooner; this is impressive." I made my way back to where he was, a seating area with plush couches and tables for study. I realized his library might contain some clues I would need in this journey. "Most impressive. You may not be the only reason I'm here." His eyebrow cocked in that handsome-yet-sinister way, and I realized he was about to ask me the reasons for the second time. I held up a hand to silence him.

"I am completely mortal right now, Vlad. My magic was stripped from me."

Dracula froze, and I almost walked over and poked him, but then his eyes caught mine, and I got lost in them. "Holy shit, you're telling the truth. I could compel you if I... if I wanted to."

I sighed. I had hoped that wouldn't be the case. His stutter, though, had him wary. "I thought as much."

"You shouldn't have come here. The reason we worked so well together was that I didn't have to control myself around you. Unfortunately, you're bringing all the emotional baggage back, and I don't want it." Vlad's eyes glistened with years of holding back tears and I almost reached out to him.

"You were a horrible woman, Medea." I nodded, realizing the floodgates were about to open. "I bared my heart to you, my soul. I gave you everything you could ever have wanted. A home, love, friendship, an ear that did not judge you on your past crimes." I hung my head in shame. "And how did you repay me? You left me. I am the most powerful vampire in history, and *you* decided to leave *me*."

"Second," I muttered softly, not thinking as my response escaped my lips.

"What?" He questioned, a dark timbre ringing through his voice. My head snapped up as a tone of command pushed through.

I gulped and looked up at him, into those black eyes which now held nothing for me. "You are the second most powerful vampire in the world." I hated to remind him of his sire, especially now, yet *that* vampire was a threat I was not ready to deal with, certainly not without Vlad on my side.

A deep, ungrateful snarl drew forth from Vlad's lips, perfectly curved as they were in hatred. The arms of his ancient chair snapped under his fingers as he held himself back. I cringed back into my corner of the couch. He loathed to be reminded of his sire... and here I was bringing it up.

"Second most powerful..." Vlad grated out through clenched teeth, "and telling me this, while I'm already upset with you is a poor choice on your part."

I gulped, trying not to draw attention to my breathing, my heartbeat, my mortality. "I'm sorry."

"You're what?" A flash of shock crossed his face before his features settled back into their normal impassive place.

"I'm sorry, Vlad, that I hurt you. I left without saying a word. I wrote you a Dear John and had Kide deliver it. I loved you, and I left you. I'm sorry. I would ..." I took another deep breath and watched as realization dawned on Drac's face. I dropped to my knees and bowed my head in shame. "I would give you my life. I *could* give you my life if I thought it would repay the damage I caused. I am sorry."

I didn't look up at him; I just kept my head down. I didn't want to see the hatred and disdain on his face. This was something I had regretted as soon as I'd done it. Just as soon as I'd realized what had gone on with Kide. But I couldn't take it back. "I'm not trying to undo what I've done, Drac; I can't do that. All I can do is make amends. In whatever way you see fit. I put my being into your hands."

A loud growl escaped from Dracula's lips, one I hadn't heard in five centuries, and he backed up away from me almost as quickly, as if I were made of garlic. "You can't offer me that. I am not a good man. I would take you, take your life, in the blink of an eye, for all the hurts you placed upon what serves as my soul."

I stood up, keeping my eyes down. I had spent years among the supernatural. I knew what to do and walked towards him. He didn't run away, and when I reached him, I placed my hands gently on his arms.

"I'm sorry, old friend. I would leave if I could, I swear it. I would go away and never trouble you again. But I was guided here." I finally looked up at him, and what I saw confused me.

Dracula's eyes were red, blood red. I saw the strain my presence had on him, and I backed away quickly, but I remembered the vampiric speed which he possessed: he was faster. Drac caught me and just held me, staring down at me.

"What do you mean, *guided* here?"

I gulped. He was one of the few supernatural beings that knew I was still in contact with my deceased sons. I occasionally used my mirror at his request to check on those he had lost in the past. My voice dropped regardless, and I sighed. "My boys."

Dracula didn't release his hold on me, but his voice softened measurably.

"They told you to come here?"

I nodded as Drac released me, but I didn't move; I just placed a hand on his cheek. "They told me to *start* with you. And I'm glad that I did. What

I did, how I hurt you, it was my lowest point in modern history." I felt him lean into my hand, and I closed my eyes. "I need to make amends; I need to fix what I broke. I want," I choked the words out, "I want your forgiveness, although I do not deserve it."

Dracula pulled my hand away from his cheek and kissed my wrist softly. I thought for a moment that he would lose control, and as he paused, I caught a flash of concern in his eyes, but he kissed it again and then held it in his hand. "Stay until you figure out your next step, Medea."

His voice was so soft. I almost didn't hear him.

"If you don't think having me will be uncomfortable. What about your wives? Do you still have some around?"

I could tell I'd hit a sore subject, but Drac never let go of my hand. "It's just the staff and me, so you will be perfectly safe. Well, as safe as a mortal can be in the house of a vampire."

I snorted. "As safe as I was five hundred years ago. You know me, and I know you. And just because my blood smells differently doesn't mean I'm not safe. I trust you." As I said the words, Dracula's hand tightened on mine. Not painfully so, but almost there.

"You, trust me..." He muttered. I felt his anguish; this was hard for him, me being here, what I've said to him, everything.

"Implicitly. You also know my boundaries, Vlad; they haven't changed." He gulped, and I smiled softly. "I'm not asking to jump into your bed or your heart. All I'm asking is that you give me a chance to make things right. I just don't know how to do that. Not right now."

Drac looked down. There was a hunger in his eyes I hadn't seen in forever, but not for blood or murder. For *me*.

"Stay here, with me, for a while. Research, relax. Whatever you need, my staff will attend to." His words were focused and careful, almost as if he had practiced them for the last five centuries–and knowing him, he had. He was as meticulous now as he was then in his preparation for every instance.

Well, almost every one.

"But that's–"

"That is what I want currently. Well, part of it." He cut me off, and I looked up at him again, dark eyes shining down at me. "The rest, we'll see. Now, shall I show you around my house, or did you want to stay in the library and read?"

I smiled brightly and laced my fingers into his. "Show me this mansion of yours; you know I like a big house that isn't mine."

Dracula just laughed and guided me on a tour of his lavish mansion, pointing out relics he thought I'd know and trying to gloss over a few that he shouldn't have obtained; his stories about his criminal activities were always filled with entertaining, enthralling anecdotes.

When the day was done, and we were back in the library and enjoying each other's conversation, it felt almost like old times, but I knew in my heart of hearts that even if Vlad forgave me, I never would. Hurting this man had broken a part of me and had damaged my relationship with Kide in irreparable ways. But I swore, as I sipped wine and laughed at his beautifully corny jokes, that I would do everything in my power to ease that burden on him because Drac was worth it, as an old lover and as a friend.

III
STUDYING THE PAST TO FIX THE FUTURE

I curled into what became my favourite place in the library: a massive, dark brown couch near the fireplace, a couch with cloud-soft cushions that resembled a swanky hotel's mattresses, and pulled open the thick, leather-bound book beside me. It was the third time I'd read through it, but every time I finished, I felt as though I had missed something. As a result, I would put it down and come back to it at a later time.

It was later, and back into my hands the book went.

Rain lashed against the windows, the thunder's rolling shook Drac's manse right down to the foundations; it was such an old house and I thought it would crumble beneath us. The fire helped to keep the chill out of my bones. Drac had rightly surmised that I was accustomed to my inner fire over the long millennia; without it, I had shown a tendency to shiver, even while wearing heavy robes. I knew from years of study that if I didn't acclimate properly, I could get extremely sick from the cooler body temperature, consequently I spent as much time near the fire as possible. The temperature wasn't as high as I used to run, and I could leave it to wean off the heat. Kide would laugh if he knew, but I'd kept this out of our texts.

I heard the door close and looked over. Dracula had returned from some function he'd had for work, his tie pulled down, and shirt unbuttoned. His dark hair was tousled, as if he had just rolled out of bed. I felt my heart tug a little when his eyes met mine, and I glanced back at the hefty tome in my hands. I tried not to pay attention as he made his way across the library, his charisma and allure, dripping from him. Dracula practically oozed charm, and a soft moan escaped my lips before he coughed gently.

"Yes, Vlad?" I asked calmly, belying the desire bubbling in my stomach.

"Is everything alright? That's the third time you've read that book. And," he paused before sitting down on the couch beside me.

"And what?" My voice dropped seductively. It wasn't something I did intentionally, but these last couple of weeks had been difficult. When I woke up screaming from the nightmares that had ravaged my mind, I sensed his presence on the other side of the door, but he did not enter. I had wanted to run into his arms so he could comfort and love me, but I didn't get up. I wouldn't open these old wounds. Wounds that I inflicted. This was my lot in life, to harm those I loved the most. I didn't love Dracula anymore; I couldn't love Dracula anymore.

This was the lie I told myself. Damn him! Damn me!

Our eyes met again as he answered my question carefully.

"You moaned a little," he said, his stare strong. I bit my lip unconsciously; I couldn't shake off the eye contact. Our gazes were riveted together. "It was unexpected."

I could tell that wasn't the answer he had planned to give, yet it was still the truth. "There is something about this book," I said, trying to pull the conversation away from anything resembling hormonal talk, "that blocks me from remembering something, and I keep reading it to figure out what it is."

"And the moan?" he prodded gently, sliding over a little.

My breath hitched, trying not to send my mind where it had the tendency to automatically go in this situation, but that was the wrong response. I easily saw the primal hunger in Drac's eyes; not to feed on my blood, but to overpower me with his lust. I grew hyper-aware of my movements, and my lips felt as dry as Death Valley in the dead of winter. I fought back my primal urge to lick them, to bring moisture to them, as I remembered just how much Drac enjoyed licking my lips in the old days.

"You're radiating charm and poise and arousal," I answered cautiously, but even I noticed the flirtatious glint on my tongue. "You haven't changed one iota."

Drac's face lit up in a smile, sheepish and cute. "Today at the studio got me thinking about things. There was someone who reminded me a lot of you in the early days." I cocked my eyebrow up at him inquiringly. "Flirtatious, yet cold. You didn't want to open up, and it took centuries to get you to warm to me."

I guffawed a little, almost ashamed. "It did not take centuries," I started, but Drac just placed a finger over my lips. Even with a fire roaring behind the grate, I felt the chill from his bloodless digit seep as far into my core as possible. He knew just how to control my emotions; a simple touch had the power to render me speechless.

And again, he had done it. I had felt his powers permeate my flesh, into my soul–and much like I had centuries prior, I had surrendered to it.

"It did, and that's ok because we got there. I'm not angry with it, not anymore." I looked at him, my eyebrow rising a mere millimeter. "Meeting this woman, having to be charming for her and the directors, exhausted me mentally. I thought I'd turned it off when I left the studio." The finger on my lips slid down, and his hand cupped my cheek. "I'm sorry I hit you with it. I swore I wouldn't do that now that you're vulnerable to it."

He leaned in quickly, not supernaturally fast, just regular human speed fast, and kissed me. Vlad's favored dark roast hung on his lips, and there was just a hint of copper dangling off a fleck of dead skin. He must have fed recently; if I really cared to look at the obits, it would be simple to find out his victim's identity — but I didn't. Not at all. I felt my heart melting the way it had years ago, but I stopped and pressed softly on his chest.

I needed to regain control. Somehow.

"I can't; I can't hurt you again, Drac. We both know I'll be leaving once I have the next step, and who knows when or if I'll ever be back," I said as softly as possible. I didn't want to hurt him again, nor did I want to hurt myself.

"I know that, Medea; believe me, I do. But I also know that I can't keep fighting these feelings, even if we're together for only a short time." His voice was as soft as mine had been, as smooth as cream, and I heard the ring of truth in it. "The woman I spoke of made me realize just how far you came when we were together and how far you've come since then. So, don't stop growing. Find love. If not with me, then with someone. You deserve it."

"As do you!" I jumped in, emphasizing the point by leaning forward and wrapping my hands into his collar. I felt like pulling him toward me–for what, only the Goddesses knew–and I started to before he spoke again.

"For me, there will only be you. My brides have all left, abandoned me, or I put them down for their crimes." My jaw hung open, and I felt rooted to the couch, unable to move as he confessed, but he continued. "I know you won't hurt me this time, because I know what's coming. I can only hope you won't forget me or our time together when you leave."

I broke at his words. Everything I had felt, everything I'd held back, evaporated. I pulled his face to mine, wrapped my hands around his neck, and planted a heavy kiss on the old vampire, sending it deep into what remained of his soul. I heard him gasp slightly, and then his hands blindly moved the book onto the table beside us. Once he finished, I felt his hands wrap around my back, pulling me up and into his lap. My legs slid onto either side of his, and I felt our desire grow. It wasn't just lust, either; this felt like two souls ripped asunder, finding their way home again.

"Vlad, I-" I started, but he bit down on my lip, pulling me back into the passion as I cried in ecstasy. I don't know why I had subconsciously decided to fight him. Fight this. I wanted him more now than I had centuries ago. I slid his tie off and pulled his suit jacket over his shoulders. Dracula wasted no time running his hand up the back of my shirt, pulling it up with the movement. I gasped, leaning back into his hands as the cool air hit my skin. As Vlad pulled my shirt over my head, he wrapped his arms around me again, embracing me tightly.

The touch felt more loving and less desperate than before, but it still held the need from which we both clung. I ripped open his shirt as if it had been made of delicate-yet-tearable fabric, hearing the buttons pop and scatter from the break, and before he could complain, my mouth claimed his, and we melted together. I could feel the desire building like a fire roaring through me and enjoyed the cool touch of his skin beneath mine.

"Medea," Drac pulled back gently, still a hair's breadth away. I just looked at him, pouring love into my eyes. "I will not stop if we get started. I don't want to. But I want to make sure you want this, too."

I replied by pulling what remained of his shirt and jacket off in one quick movement, my lips seeking the hollow of his neck, just below his earlobe. "Don't ask stupid questions, love. I'm not going anywhere, and I'm not stopping this." Even though I was a part of this, I felt disbelief in hearing how much I sounded like a horny twenty-something human. My voice had a husky overtone, heady with feral desire, and Drac's hands were pressed against my back, moving across my skin with a genuine delight.

I felt him shudder beneath me and rocked up on my knees a little, my hands running down his chest, up his arms, anywhere my fingers reached. The pool of heat building between us was not something I was avoiding. I just wanted to savor this moment. The passion hadn't died between us like I feared it might; if anything, it was stronger. The kiss was deep, pulling me under the spell we had woven. This magic was intrinsic, innate—intimate. There was no casting or words necessary, only the depth of our love and the joy in our hearts.

I don't know how long we were there, just kissing, breathing each other in, drinking in the firelight, but I didn't care. I wasn't hungry or tired; I just wanted this: this connection with Vladimir Dracul, my first genuine love after Jason, my only real love after him. Pulling out of the kiss, I looked down at his dark, piercing black eyes. Eyes that drew me in both willingly and unwillingly. I spoke the words I had feared to say for centuries. Words I hadn't even said when we were together. "I love you, Vladimir Dracul. With my entire being, I love you."

Surprise and delight sparkled in his eyes, and I felt one hand wind into my hair while the other wrapped around my waist. "As I love you, Medea, regardless of our past, shared and separate. I always will."

What remaining willpower I had dissipated, and I whispered gently to him, licking up his neck and nibbling on his earlobe. "Make love to me, Dracula. Make me believe that the world is just us; there is nothing else."

He looked up at me and bit my lip again. I slid one hand under his pants, worked the belt and zipper loose with the other one, and felt him spring up to meet me.

Dracula nodded and hiked my skirt up around my waist. He pushed my soaking lace panties aside and grazed two fingers across my clit, causing me to gasp and lean backwards. I stroked him slowly, our hands moving together as one, and Drac's free hand rested on my back to prevent me from falling. As we progressed, gradually caressing each other tenderly, I forgot why I was even here. I forgot I had left him. I only remembered that I loved him and that he was mine as much as I was his.

We worked his pants down to fully expose him, and I smiled, biting my lip again. I forgot how thick he was. Once again, his eyes met mine when I positioned myself above him. Lowering down on him, I gasped in delight. The feeling of his cock spreading me open sent swirls of pleasure through my whole body. "Oh, gods!" I cried out, our fingers clasping together as I settled down over him. We held a moment, letting my body adjust, and then slowly began dancing.

It was a dance we were familiar with, having mastered the steps eons ago, but there was something fresh, something new about this. We swayed up, crashed down, tilted sideways, but always together, always as one. Our eyes never left the others, and I could feel something changing, something growing. Our lips hovered over the others, and we breathed in each other's air. Time stopped, even more than it had previously. I felt Drac shudder and heard him groan. I knew he felt it too.

We were becoming one again. Mind, body, soul: a perfect partnership. I didn't think this could be, especially not with my past, but I knew in my gut, Drac was my future, so long as I survived this trial of fire.

"Medea," he croaked, his voice almost imperceptibly soft. I nodded, unable to speak for the moans and gasps that escaped my lips. "I'm almost there, are you?" I nodded again and felt his nails dig into my skin gently. This sex was right at the top of my Top 10 list, and I knew we weren't done for the night.

"I'm ready, my Dracula," I replied softly, and I clenched around him in proof. My legs had turned into jelly a while ago, and Vlad just smiled.

"Good." As he replied, I felt the heat burst from within us, filling the emptiness and spilling down our legs. Dracula growled darkly, and I shivered as the orgasm kept ripping through us. Then, as the wave broke, I felt a click, like a tumbler in a lock, and smiled unknowingly.

I rested my head on his shoulder as we came down from the high and noticed a secondary glow in the room, one that wasn't emanating from the hearth or the windows. I looked at the table where Drac had placed the tome and saw it shining with orange light. He reached over and picked it up, flipping the book open and resting it on the couch beside us. I hadn't removed myself from him, and he hadn't tried to pull me off either.

When I looked down, something fell into place.

Love shall be your guide, your soul to rend and mend, beware the abysmal pit, the mirror forth shall send.

I stared at it. I had never seen these words before, and yet I knew that this was what my mind couldn't grasp. "Well fuck me," I muttered.

"I thought I just had," Drac's eyes twinkled.

I chuckled and slapped his chest gently. "I meant, if I'm reading this right, I'm heading to Tartarus. And," I gulped, "you'll be the one to take me."

IV
THE MOST MAGICAL
NON-MAGIC NIGHT
OF MY LIFE

Tartarus, the one place in all creation that I didn't want to visit, but the one place I knew the gods destined me for. If I hadn't sat on Drac's lap, he'd have fallen over. As it was, he tried to leap up and only drove himself further into me, causing us both to groan with pleasure.

"What do you mean, I'll be sending you there?" Dracula's voice was steely, and I withered slightly.

"No, I believe it means that you are going to accompany me... if you want." I added quickly. I didn't want to force him into anything, especially on a trip down there. "I knew my trip would take me to the Underworld. I need to see my sons without magic between us."

I sighed, got up off Drac's lap, and walked over to the fireplace. I grabbed a heavy log and, as soon as I had the grate pulled to the side, I tossed the wood deeper into the conflagration.

"I didn't know I'd be going to Tartarus during the trip. Unless it means I fail." I muttered under my breath.

Dracula was behind me in an instant, spinning me around and pinning me to the wall. "I will *not* allow you to fail, Medea." He glared down at me, and I thought he would enchant me for a moment, but then Drac placed his head on my shoulder, and I felt him shake. "I can't give you my heart and have you die on me. I won't allow it. If I must walk every step of the journey with you to make sure you live, I will."

I stopped breathing for a moment. Bringing him with me was an option I hadn't considered, mainly because Kide and I would have to travel overland or by translocation most of the way. Also, I didn't know if Kide had it within him to manage another passenger.

"I don't want you in danger, Vlad. I... I couldn't live with myself if you died while protecting me because the gods know I can't do it at the moment."

He cupped my face in his hands and lifted it to look at him once more. I stared and felt my heart crumble, the pain behind his gaze as evident as his long-held love for me.

"And if you died while on this trip, and I knew I could have been there? I will stake myself if that happens, Medea. You are stuck with me, and I am coming with you."

I stared up at him, numb, then nodded. He held me there, pinned to the wall, and just kissed me. I fell into it. It was magical, and I don't use that term often, but I used it now. As I felt the last of my walls breaking down, I knew this was necessary. I needed to heal him and have him heal me in return. I would never break his heart again, lest I destroy my own.

"Can you go to your room in a minute?" he whispered. "There is a surprise for you waiting on your bed. And then meet me back here?"

I looked up, curious, but his dark eyes only sparkled at me. "As you wish, my love. I'll be back shortly." He leaned off the wall and sped away quickly. I could never hope to catch him, at least, not without Kide here, and that was okay. I pushed myself off the wall slowly, half in a daze, and walked back to my room. When I got there, I found the door open, with a sleek black dress lying on the bed. Dracula wrote the note that rested on top of the dress. I recognized his fine penmanship, even at a distance.

Medea,

If you would be so inclined, I would like you to join me for dinner. You and me, no one else. No staff, no Kide, just us. Like a date. I would take you on a proper date if you wish, but please join me tonight.

I remain yours, humbly,

Vladimir Dracul

I picked the dress up, and I felt my eyes sparkle as I let my gaze stray across the impressive fabric. Spider silk was relatively scarce these days, the quantities needed to craft even a single garment took years to cultivate, and no one kept spider gardens anymore. I held it up to the light and reveled in how luxurious it felt beneath my fingers and how it reflected the meagre light. I stripped quickly and stood there for a moment, just feeling the dress.

A text interrupted me, and I looked down at my phone. It was Kide, but I would get back to him after dinner. I slid the dress on and damned near had an orgasm as it fit to my figure. It was perfect: black silk that clung to and teased every inch of me. It felt more like a slip than a dress, something I would have worn under formal attire a few centuries ago.

I looked in the mirror. The black lace scalloped trim above my cleavage was classy and yet left nothing to the imagination. The dress ended mid-thigh, with some lace decoration on the bottom. I paired it with a nice pair of strappy red heels, a little colour to catch the eye. I spent a short time fixing my hair and putting on some make-up... not that I had much to begin with, but I wanted to look my best.

After a few more minutes of ogling myself from above, I twirled in front of the mirror before heading out. As I made my way back to the library, the change caught me by surprise. Vlad had set a table up near the fireplace, and had placed candelabras all over the room, giving the library a magical glow. In the center of the room stood Vlad Dracul, in a deep crimson suit cut perfectly to his figure. The crimson was his preferred colour. I walked over, and he bowed gracefully.

"How did you get this all done?"

Drac strolled towards me and took my hand, bending forward slightly to kiss it. Such a smooth seductionist. "I move quickly."

I blushed furiously and nodded. "You do; I also know you know how to move slowly when necessary." It was Drac's turn to blush. Well, the pale skin on his cheeks darkened slightly, and I smiled. "You didn't make all this food, Drac. Where did it come from?" I asked, as he guided me to the table and pulled out my chair.

As I sat down, and he pushed it in, Drac replied. "The chefs had been preparing it. I will not lie and say that I haven't had this ready for a while, just in case." He sat down beside me and opened a bottle of red. The bouquet caught my nose, and I recognized the year.

"I thought you said some five hundred years ago that you only had one of those bottles," I commented lightly as he poured the wine into a decanter, letting it breathe more.

"Ah, my love, you misheard. I said I had one left." I chuckled softly as we started into the meal. The artichoke heart appetizer was delicious, but the main course, bacon-wrapped filet mignon, which the chefs cooked to a perfect medium-rare, with steamed vegetables, roasted garlic mashed potatoes, and some fettuccine alfredo, had my mouth watering. I almost skipped the appetizers, but once I put the first artichoke heart into my mouth, I forgot what I was doing. The chefs in this time were unparalleled, and I sank into the chair.

"Is it good?" he asked.

I looked up at him and smiled brightly. "It is. Please, my compliments to the chef. Kide and I, we normally don't eat this well. Well, we haven't in quite a while." I remembered the text on my phone and shook my head. I silently reminded myself to check it later. We talked a little as we ate. We just enjoyed the food and each other's company. Without thinking, as I nibbled on the steak, I reached over and took Drac's hand in mine, intertwining our fingers. It wasn't until Drac got up to get the dessert that I realized he was taking my hand with him.

"Oh, sorry."

I couldn't help but blush.

"It's alright, my dear. I will gladly hold on to it when I get back, but I need two hands to bring out the dessert." I chuckled again and nodded, getting up to help him bring the dishes into the kitchen. But a couple of his staff appeared quickly and took them all away. I sat back down, crossed my legs, and took a long sip of the wine. It was delicious and potent, with a dark red, almost blood-like colour. I reached for the bottle and read the year: 1666, a year which has been remembered as hard for a lot of supernatural beings, but it somehow produced one of the best crops of wine I had ever tasted. I poured us both another glass as Drac came back with a large trifle.

"Do you expect both of us to eat that?" I joked lightly.

He laughed with me and placed it down on the table. "I couldn't care less if we ate it all tonight or if we woke up in the morning and had it for breakfast. I made it for you."

I looked at it. Angel food cake, fresh fruit, whipped cream, and custard, all blended and stacked to perfection. I felt a rumbling coming from somewhere near my feet. How the hell was I still hungry, after I had eaten enough for three of me?

"Would you care for some?" Vlad asked. I nodded. How could I not? Vlad served up a mountainous helping of the trifle and passed its weight over.

"Thank you, Vlad, for everything." He looked at me, dark eyes sparkling in the candlelight, and I continued. "For letting me into your home, for letting me stay. For healing my heart when I wasn't trying to do that." I gulped as I watched what served as the intake of breath. "For offering to come with me, even though we both know the rest of my journey will be dangerous."

"That's why I offered..." he muttered, but I held up a hand to silence him.

I continued.

"For letting me back in, Drac. I thank the gods for you, even though they cursed me to live as a mortal. I thank them for you."

Dracula stood up quickly and pulled me up to him; our trifles left uneaten.

"You. Beautiful. Little. Witch," he punctuated his words with kisses, each one growing more and more passionate. I leaned in, my arms wrapping around his neck, and smiled. "You are filling my heart every day. I'd forgotten how lonely it was without you. And," he paused, placed his hands on my cheeks and made sure I was looking at him, "If you don't let me come with you, I will follow you anyway. Nothing felt right after you left, and now? I can't go back to how it was."

I stared at him, the intensity in his eyes. I saw that he struggled in his desire to not compel me. He wouldn't need to. I needed him with me, as much as he needed me. I realized this, and he had, too.

"I couldn't stop you, Drac, even if I wanted to, which I don't. I don't want to go back to how it was, either. You are like coming up for air when, for centuries, I was drowning."

Drac pulled me back into a kiss, and there was no resistance. So, this was us; this was everything. His hands snaked down my back and hooked under my ass, picking me up effortlessly. I wrapped my legs around him, and he carried us out of the library and up to his room. It had been centuries since I'd been in his room, but it was the same style as the one in Transylvania. He set me down on the bed, leaning over me hungrily. I shivered under his gaze, and the only question he asked was low and husky.

"What is off the table?"

"Nothing, Vlad, nothing."

I had meant it, and there was a reason why I had meant it: during our first tryst, back when I had a full array of magical powers and talents and that pesky thing called immortality at my disposal, there was one thing, just one, that Dracula would never hope to achieve. He could never feed on me. I held sun fire in my hands, and I would never risk his life on the chance.

But now? I was mortal. 'They' snuffed the fire out, and I wanted him to sink his teeth in. I needed to feel it, and I wasn't sure why. Maybe it's because it's one of the few things we had never done before; perhaps it's because we finally could. I reached up, placed my hands on his face, and guided him down to my neck, leaning to the opposite side.

"Medea!" The shock in his voice almost broke the spell of the evening, but I shushed him and nodded, looking at Dracula to reassure him that I meant what I said. I felt his willpower break, and then fangs pierced my skin. I gasped at once. The venom he injected into my skin through his fangs coursed through my veins; I felt myself weaken with desire. I knew this happened, but I had never experienced it, and holy fuck! The sensation was orgasmic. I now knew why people wanted a vampire to feed on them. This sensation had the potential to turn addictive, like an opiate. Dracula locked his fingers with mine, and I felt him spasm as he drank me in. I didn't stop him; I didn't want to.

I gasped a little, and Dracula disengaged his fangs from my neck, then licked the wound to stop the bleeding. He leaned up, looking down at me. I do not know what he saw in my eyes, but his lips were on mine in an instant, and nothing else mattered. This, in his arms, was where I was happiest, and I would kill anyone who tried to take it away.

The night melted away; we fell into our delirium, growing lost in desire, succumbing to lust.

V
PLACATING THE COLCHIAN DRAGON

There are few things in the world that will startle me awake from the rested, satisfied slumber I now experienced; sex with a vampire will certainly satisfy a person. Those things generally include thinking I left the stove on, why the tip of a shoelace has an actual name—it's an aglet—and the assorted reasons why I know this, the nightmare of my infanticide, and the ever-present reality of my life.

But on this early evening, I added a new one to the list: realizing that I, Medea of Colchis, Protector of the Golden Fleece, Mistress of Potions, etc, added a new title that I didn't necessarily want to get out.

That title was Leaver of Texts Unread.

And how, pray tell, did I gain this horrific title? It was when I saw a rather familiar-looking dragon soar through the sky, magical wards be damned all to Hell, to engage in a brutal assault of Dracula's manor.

I rolled out of bed, suddenly wide awake as Vlad's alarm system, a set of heavy gongs and cloisters, hit poignant notes. Looking around, I found Dracula in fighting mode, fangs out and nails extended. I watched his eyes scan the room. Nothing was in the immediate vicinity, but as I looked out the window, a giant blue-black dragon slammed into the wards.

"Shit! I forgot Kide's text!" I took off down the hall to my room, throwing on some clothing quickly before heading outside. I slipped down the wet stairs, falling onto my ass, and began screaming into the air.

"Kide! KIDEMONOS!! Drac, can you let down your wards?"

The vampire was right behind me and shook his head.

"You put them up, Medea; you cursed him. Even I can't fix that."

I sighed. I thought as much. Kide hadn't tried burning the place down yet, so I waved my arms at him.

"Kide! I'm here. I'm ok!" I yelled.

That time, he heard me. Kide's boulder-sized head jerked toward us. I felt my lungs inflate sharply, just before he let out a roar that resembled a kitten's mew. I felt two black eyes fixate on me, and at that point, I had to go to him. I ran to the open gate.

I didn't expect Vladimir to follow me. I expected him to stay behind, to stay as close to the protection his manor gave him. After all, Kide and Dracula didn't necessarily get along, and both men had the scars to prove it.

But he did. And surprisingly, he took my hand as we exited his property.

Kide settled on the ground in front of us and huffed loudly. *Well. I'm glad you are alright, Medea.* The tone of his voice told me he had thought otherwise until this moment. His eyes focused on my hand, fingers interlocked with Dracula's, and I watched as the twenty-foot dragon finally morphed from reptile to the form of a six-foot six-inch man.

"Oh, Medea. I hope... I hope this will not be like last time," He sighed and placed his hands on my shoulders. "Are you sure?"

I nodded.

He looked at Dracula. I watched as invisible hands straightened both men's backs.

"And you, I expect you to treat her like the goddess she is."

"Better, sir, I will not risk losing her a second time," Dracula replied earnestly. I squeezed his hand, and he looked at me, smiling.

"Kide, I'm sorry I didn't answer your text last night. Drac and I had a little date night," I explained quickly.

"It's alright. I wanted to inform you. I know where we're going next," Kide replied.

My mouth fell open.

"You do? How?"

"It was odd. Yesterday evening, I felt this warmth seep into my heart. It felt like your heartfire, Medea, and suddenly I had this vision of Aetna," Kide responded. I watched as he fidgeted and remembered the last time we were in Sicily. This would not be pretty.

I reached out and took Kide in my arms, hugging him tightly. As much as this journey was about healing me, Kide and I existed in one body most of the time. My struggles were his and vice versa. So, this next stop would not be about me; it would be about Kide.

"It's alright. We'll get through this, I promise."

Dracula just stood back and looked at us. "What is wrong with Aetna? Sicily is a beautiful island."

I nodded and smiled softly.

"It is gorgeous, and I spent a couple of centuries there not long before I came to you. But, unfortunately, Kide had," I looked up into the dragon's eyes, and he nodded, "he had a falling out of sorts with Hephaestus, or Vulcan, if you will."

I sensed Dracula trying not to laugh, and the dragon in my arms bristled.

"You fell out with a god?!"

I turned to look at Drac and watched him wither under my gaze.

"That was uncalled for, and if you are going to take pot-shots at Kide, you can stay here."

His mouth fell open, but in true Dracula fashion, he recovered quickly.

"Even if you did, I would follow you."

"He's *not* coming with us, Medea, is he?" Kide asked, incredulous.

I blushed and looked up at my oldest friend. "Yes, he is... He, we..." Fuck, it disconcerted me. I did not need to be, and yet here I am. "Yesterday afternoon, we opened our hearts to each other. I admitted what I never could, centuries ago. When we first joined," I looked at Dracula, and he smiled sheepishly, "when we reached our orgasm together, the tome I had been stuck on for weeks suddenly glowed and a new passage was visible."

Kide's eyes widened and held me back to look at me properly.

"What did it say, this passage?"

I looked up at him and whispered. *"Love shall be your guide, your soul to rend and mend, beware the abysmal pit, the mirror forth shall send."*

Kide's arms fell to his sides, and he stepped back. The realization had settled.

"Tartarus..." Kide's black eyes roared with a fire I'd not seen before, and I jumped back, Drac wrapping his arms around me. "I swear it, Medea, I will not let you go there. You won't return from the Pit."

"I know," I muttered. My willpower about this whole excursion had slowly eroded, and now that I knew the next steps were to confront Hephaestus, I knew just how bad things were going to get. Kide and I had spent centuries running, hiding, using people when we needed to so that the Furies wouldn't come calling again. "Anyway," I shook my head, clearing my thoughts, and smiled, "how are we getting to Italy? Can you teleport us all the way there?"

Kide smirked and then shook his head. "No, I can't, but I would like to ask you if you would be okay flying?"

I cocked my eyebrow at him, and Kide continued.

"I know you and I fly all the time, or we did, but... if we're heading to Sicily, I need time to think about my next steps. So maybe, if Dracula is coming..." he left the question hanging, but Dracula understood.

"I'll book us a flight out tomorrow. Then we can meet up in Sicily when you're ready," Dracula replied.

I looked over at Kide.

"When will you meet us? I don't enjoy travelling separately." I saw that it scared him, being separated. I was afraid, too.

"A week from now, I'll meet you in Adrano. I promise." With that, Kide kissed my forehead, formed his great wings without resuming his full draconic shape, and then took off. The blast of wind knocked me back into Vlad's arms. Part of me worried he wouldn't face this next challenge, but all I could do was trust my oldest friend.

Dracula put his arm around me, and immediately I felt better, safer. We made our way back into the manor, and I stopped at the doorway.

"It's the middle of the day. How are you outside?" I asked. I couldn't believe I hadn't noticed it before.

Drac wheeled me inside as his laughter erupted once again.

"I met an angel once, a few years after you left." He guided me down the hallways and back into the bedroom. "I was sad, angry, depressed. I wanted it all to go away." His lips met my neck, and his hands slowly peeled my clothing. I breathed a soft smile. "I attacked, intent on the thought that he would kill me, but he didn't." Dracula lifted me and pinned me to the wall. "One drop of his blood on my lips and I could walk in the sunlight, a blessing I never thought I needed, but one I am grateful for now."

He had wriggled his pants down, and I felt him pressing up against me.

"How did you overpower an angel?"

I was curious, I'll admit it.

Dracula teased me, and I felt myself grow sodden.

He finally answered.

"I honestly do not know. Maybe he was already wounded by something. Maybe I was stronger than I thought." He rocked his hips up towards mine, slamming into me. I screamed out as he continued. "Either way, I can live a semi-normal life now, not confined to my house, the night, and the dreary cloud-filled days. I can enjoy the sunlight again."

With every sentence, he thrust up into me, filling every inch of me with him.

"Oh, gods... whoever that angel is, or was... I owe them a debt of gratitude!"

Dracula grabbed my hair and pulled back, rough and yet loving. "I can enjoy the Italian countryside; I can enjoy *you* in the Italian countryside now," he growled. His lips hadn't left my neck, and I nodded, leaning away again.

"Whenever you need it, my love, all of me is for you," I mumbled before I felt his fangs sink into my flesh again. I damn near burst from the ecstasy it brought. As he fed, I fell into the venom, letting it flow through me, my mind growing hazy. Beyond Dracula, there was nothing else. "Did you want to pick up the arrangement we had last time?" I asked, my voice barely above a whisper.

Dracula finished drinking and licked the wounds closed before pulling back and looking at me. He held me in place, cock twitching within, and smiled. "Do you want to, my little witch?"

I groaned softly and pulled him into a deep kiss.

"If I didn't, I wouldn't have asked."

Dracula shuddered and nodded.

"We'll need to rework the contract, though. Some things are now null-and-void, and others now exist."

I chuckled softly and nodded.

"Of course. But first, I have a question for you." Dracula's black eyes met mine, and I saw flecks of silver dancing in them. He was playful today. He gave me a slow nod and began thrusting again. "Can I cum now, please?" I croaked out.

"Oh, good girl, you remembered." He paused and picked up the pace, placing his thumb under my chin gently. I waited for my answer, hoping it would come soon. "Yes, Medea, my Medea, you may cum."

At the word 'yes,' I exploded violently, pushing down on him with everything I had; I had the feeling that I had just soaked his legs. Dracula growled fiercely, and I shivered beneath him. It was a sound I loved, one that drenched me instantly. He pulled me off the wall and carried me to the bed, putting me down gently. I was panting. The orgasm shook me that hard, and yet, I knew we weren't finished. Dracula leaned up, pushed all the way in and brought his lips down to mine.

"I am going to have you in as many ways as possible tonight. We can work out the contract on the flight to Catania tomorrow, but for now, as long as we agree on where we were last time," I nodded, "then I plan to have you for hours and hours."

I groaned and bit his lower lip.

"Then do with me what you will, milord." I felt him grow within me, and I moaned loudly.

"Oh, I will," Dracula joined me in orgasm, and I felt him fill me with his seed. It was a feeling I sorely missed and one I would never get used to. He dragged himself up and kissed down my body. As Dracula reached my thigh, he grazed his fangs over my clit, causing me to jump. "My good girl, my good, perfect, little girl." A kiss followed each word, and at the end, Drac rolled my right leg slightly and sank his fangs in.

I gasped. My eyes rolled back in my head as he worked with his fingers, which had moved into my pussy and ass. "Leave a mark, please, when you feed." I groaned out, my voice a husky whisper, and I felt my love nod. "Oh, gods, Vlad!" I cried out as he began suckling the area. My clit was forgotten, yet the stimulation I was receiving brought me higher than ever before. This feeling was divine, dark, and delicious, and I did not want it to end, but as I felt the wave crest again, I remembered just in time to ask. "Please..." I whimpered softly, "I need to cum, may I?" When I felt him shake his head, I began begging. "Gods, please, I need to... Please, SIR!" I cried out.

Drac pulled his fangs out and looked at me before speaking. "Now, you may cum." His face was between my thighs again, ready to drink up a different form of elixir, and I obliged him. I squirted into his face, and Dracula drank as though his life depended on it. When he finished, he licked me clean and then smiled up at me. "Your turn."

Two simple words, and yet I longed for them. I rolled off the bed and pushed him back, pulling off his shirt quickly. My lips met his skin, and I heard a sharp intake of breath. It made me happy that I could bring him this much joy, just from my lips on his chest. I began working my way down, enjoying each contour, every line that guided me to my goal. When my lips touched his tip, Dracula shivered beneath me, and I smiled before taking him all in slowly. I knew my love wouldn't last like this. He never could. It was one of the things I loved most about him.

I felt his hands wrap into my hair, and he urged me forward; I loved it when he guided me. "Yes, Medea, right there." Dracula moaned, and I picked up the pace. He gasped as I pushed his cock down, and it only spurred me to move faster. A few minutes later, I felt him twitch again and heard him gasp. "I'm almost there, Medea, please."

I groaned around him and felt him shiver hard. Finally, it was time, and when I locked eyes with him, Dracula exploded. I drank him all, greedy for him. Then, with speed born from his vampiric powers and years of experience, Drac moved and pinned me to the bed. "Now, my little witch, are you ready for the rest of the night?"

I smiled up at him as he bound my hands to the bed and bit my lip.

"Yes, my love. I am ready for the rest of our lives."

VI
A SICILIAN
ADVENTURE

Adrano. It was a beautiful town nestled right beneath Aetna. It wasn't a typical entrance to the forges of Hephaestus, or Vulcan as he was known here, but Kide and I knew of an alternate way into and under the mountain. Dracula's rented town car had sped down the Italian highway, bringing us closer to Adrano and the mountain. Towering cypress trees lined the road, and wild olive groves and grapevines grew in the fields behind it. It looked as though nothing had changed here in the centuries since my departure. I grew more nervous with every passing mile.

Finally, Drac placed a hand on my thigh. I glanced his way and caught a caring gleam in his eye, as if he had sensed my hesitation. That one touch, however, calmed me. It was amazing how integral he had become to this trip, to my life. I quietly scolded myself for ever letting him go. I would not make that mistake again. His hand tightened slightly, and I knew his mind was where mine was, and I leaned into him, seeking his comfort.

Before us stretched a long, winding drive, cutting through acres of vineyards. We were in such gorgeous countryside and my heart grew tender with gladness to be here once again, even if the situation was less than ideal.

"What's on your mind? We're almost there, Meds, *Castello Solicchiata*," he announced as we bypassed Adrano and made our way closer to the base of the mountain. Drac's voice cut through my thoughts, and I smiled over at him.

"Just that it's been almost a thousand years since Kide and I were here. So much has changed, and yet it hasn't. Italy has this magical quality to it, where even though you see the modern world everywhere, the Old World shines through. She shows you just how majestic she was in ancient times, and I loved it. I think maybe I'll find a pleasant country home here once we take care of all this nonsense."

If I survive, I thought.

Dracula just laughed. "It certainly seems to fit you. If I didn't know your fire was gone, I'd have said you had your old glow back."

"What can I say? It feels so much like home," I replied as we pulled up in front of the house. "I didn't think this place was available to rent?" The driver got out and opened Drac's door. The fresh summer air caught my nose, bringing notes of grape, lavender, and olive to me. I stepped out after my undead beau, taking his proffered hand, and looked around. *Castello Solicchiata* was a large manor—about the size of Vlad's house in Los Angeles, but this was far more stately and well built, a real credit to the architect of the time—and I wondered what Dracula had to give up securing this place for the week.

"Shall we get settled?" Dracula smiled and wrapped his arm around my waist. I nodded. This place was breathtaking, and he wheeled us towards the front door. As we entered, the staff greeted us like royalty, and I won't lie. I enjoyed it. It had been an eon since anyone treated me with both respect and deference. I looked up at Drac, who seemed to bask in their adoration. I wondered if they knew exactly who we were. "We have the house for the week since I assume you'll want to move on to the next location once Kide fixes the bond between him and the Lame God?"

I nodded again. Something told me we were on a schedule, and even taking this week's break was pushing it. But I couldn't press Kide into facing his problems; he was just as stubborn as Hephaestus, and both had fiery tempers.

"Yes, that is likely. I wish I knew what the next steps were so I could better prepare. The mirror hasn't shown me anything recently." *Neither have my boys*, but I didn't give voice to that pain.

It must have shown on my face, though, because Dracula wrapped me in his arms and brushed his lips against my forehead gently. I shivered.

"It'll be alright, love; everything will work out. And before we know it, you'll be back to your usual fiery self."

As we did not know when Kide would arrive--I hoped he wouldn't Translocate--we took the time to make our solitude an impromptu romantic getaway; when in Italy, do what the Italians do. Although both of us could stay here all week, sequestered in this massive castle, Dracula wanted to get out and see the sights with me. How could I refuse? Adrano was such a beautiful town. I chuckled as we toured the manor, each of us pointing out places that interested us or where we thought fucking each other's brains out would be greatest.

Once we settled into our room, we slipped into more comfortable clothing: a light green sundress and sandals for me and khakis with a linen shirt for Drac, and we left to wander the town. This was how we spent our week:

exploring in the morning before the sun got too hot for us, and then we would have lunch somewhere before returning to *Castello Solicchiata*. We would then enjoy the rest of our day touring the castle, drinking wine, and keeping out of the heat.

Towards the end of the week, Dracula and I were out for dinner after an afternoon rain when a drenched Kide arrived.

"Kide!" I started. We pulled an extra chair over to the chagrin of the other patrons and the staff. I didn't care. "What happened?"

My dragon sat down and grabbed my wine. Now I knew something was wrong; Kide never drank. "I had to swim from the mainland here."

I looked at Dracula and then at Kide. "What do you mean? What..." I looked, really looked at him and gasped. "Kidemonos, where are your wings?"

Kide didn't meet my eyes; he just guzzled the wine and then grabbed the bottle. My face knit in worry. I may be without my powers, but this lack of *being* was clear, even in his human form. I pulled him to me, sliding my chair against his. "Tell me, please."

Dracula signaled for the bill as Kide shook against me. "I got to Naples, went to visit the base of Vesuvius, and..." he broke down, sobbing, "it was like someone struck me with lightning. I fell to the ground, a searing pain shooting through my back. I passed out on the side of the road. When I came to, I could feel the difference. I can shift back, but..." he shrugged, and I clasped him.

"Oh, my dear Kide." I just kept my arms around him while his sorrow poured out of him. Drac paid quickly and then picked Kide up; his vampiric strength was amazing to me. There were no words between the three of us as we walked back up to *Castello Solicchiata*. When we returned to the manor, Dracula brought Kide into the kitchen and placed the dragon down on the floor in front of the fireplace.

"Now I know how you felt, Medea, all those weeks ago, when you collapsed on the shoreline." I shuddered as the memory assaulted me. I hadn't told Dracula about the exact moment the fire left me, but my attention snapped back to Kide. "I am so sorry."

"For what, old friend? You've been nothing but supportive." I knelt beside him, holding his hands in mine.

"I didn't think it was such a big deal; your magic doesn't make you, you. That was how I was looking at it. You were still my Medea." I nodded slowly, having that internal debate myself, "but this, my wings. I am no longer a dragon. I am a *wyrm*." He practically spat the word out, and I recoiled from the venom in Kide's voice.

"For now," I retorted, understanding his frustration. "Once we get to Hephaestus, I will plead your case. The timing can't be a coincidence."

He looked up at me, cold black eyes boring into my soul. "What do you mean?" Drac cut in before Kide could snap at me. I knew my oldest friend; I knew when he was bubbling with anger.

"Think about it. I lost my powers a couple of months ago. Why didn't Kide lose his wings then?" The men looked at each other. "We only just found out the next leg of the journey was to Heph. *He* would have known ages ago, or at the very least, when all this shit started." Kide's mouth fell open, and I squeezed his hands. "You were on your way here to face your past; he knows that. Hephaestus wants to make sure you are committed to this."

"That shouldn't have ever been a question."

There was the snap. I didn't wince. I knew he didn't mean the viscera. Sighing, I pressed my forehead to his.

"Yes, because you and I are one, my *kidemonos*, but perhaps he wanted to make sure you were doing this for yourself? Or maybe he wanted to give you the incentive to come instead of just for me."

A low growl escaped his lips, and I leaned back.

"Does he really think so low of me?"

I felt Dracula's eyes bouncing between the two of us, but I replied to Kide. "You know that isn't true. You were one of his favourite students. It was my fault we left. We *both* need to pay our dues with him." I looked over at Dracula and sighed. "I will explain later, but let's get him into a room so that he can relax. The journey, plus the loss. I wish he hadn't been alone."

We helped Kide up and brought him to a room down the hall from ours. Once we settled him in and made sure Kide was dry, Drac and I retired to our room. I was drained, not from any physical exertion, but from the mental exhaustion of reconnecting with Kide and feeling his pain. I hadn't realized just how much it hurt for us to be apart. When you spend over 3,500 years with another being, and when you have the close bond that we do, separation takes a physical toll.

Finally, I collapsed, dizzier than I remembered feeling.

"Medea!" Dracula had me in his arms before I hit the ground. Soon, I felt the softness of the bed under me.

"I'm sorry, love, you've been a pack mule all evening." My voice was shaky. Dracula just curled himself around me, his arms bringing me the comfort of his love. "I feel horrible for Kide. His wings are part of him."

"Just as your magic is a part of you," he replied softly. "You both have a long way to go to get yourselves back to where you were. And now I am exceedingly glad that I'm here. Kide needs my help just as much as you do. You two have supported each other for millennia; it's time for someone else to help you out. And if that is the only reason I'm here, I am glad to do what I can."

I rolled over and looked at him, very little strength in my body, but my eyes shone with passion. "That is *not* why you're here. Well, I suppose not the only reason. I love you, Dracula, I want you here because you give me strength, and I couldn't imagine doing this without you."

Dracula's eyes sparkled at me, and his lips brushed mine. "I'm glad for that, but for now, sleep. We will plan our trip under the mountain tomorrow after you and Kide have rested."

I felt my eyes droop and wondered for the briefest moment if Drac had compelled me to sleep, but I knew in my heart that he wouldn't do that.

The next morning, I woke alone in the bed, missing the cool touch of Dracula's skin against mine. I rolled out from under the covers, changed out of my dress from the night before, and made my way to Kide's room. I knocked twice, my knuckles stinging but he didn't answer. If I had my powers, I'd just feel where his presence was and make my way over. Now, though, I had to search the old-fashioned way – like a damned human. That meant deduction and elimination. If I knew Kide, he would be outside somewhere to bask in the sun. So, I made my way downstairs and out the back to the veranda. It looked over the vast vineyard and saw the Colchian Dragon wandering among the vines, aimless and vacant. I made my way down to him, but I felt Drac's hand on my arm.

"Give him a moment. He knows you are here, dear." I looked up at him as he wrapped me in his arms, leaning his chin on my shoulder. A few minutes later, Kide joined us on the veranda and sat down beside me.

"We'll need to see him soon," Kide said softly. I nodded, sad at the turn of events.

"Can someone fill me in on what happened between you and Hephaestus?" Dracula asked, his voice barely above a whisper.

We looked at each other, and Kide nodded. I took a deep breath and smiled softly. "It was about, what, a thousand years ago?" Kide nodded again. "We had run into a spot of trouble in the forests of modern Turkey." I paused for a moment. "Fuck." Both men looked at me as realization dawned on me of where we'll be heading after this. I shook my head; I'd tell them later. "Anyway, we flew to Sicily; Kide always had a good relationship with Hephaestus and asked for temporary asylum. He was much less irritable about visitors then, than he was in the past. So, Heph let us stay as long as we wanted, so long as we helped in the forge." Kide nodded in agreement with me.

"Kide stayed under the mountain and worked with Hephaestus for, oh what, 250 years?" Kide agreed with me, and I continued. "I stayed here, in Adrano. I don't even remember what I did during that time."

"You drank a lot."

I snorted.

"Yes, well, you would, too, if you were in Italy hiding out. I remembered at the end, I crossed paths with some vampires, bloodthirsty and cruel, who were preying on the townspeople. I may have stepped in and staked a few... sorry Drac."

His mouth fell open, and I shook a little. "I'd heard about that shortly after my creation. That was you?"

"It was, yes. The clan was on the verge of wiping out Adrano. There was no one to keep them in check. The Elders were asleep." I sighed. "I don't normally step into the affairs of the other races, but this was too much and I slew every single one of them. Unfortunately, that earned the ire of their sire, and I ran to the only place I knew of for help."

"You were a 2,750-year-old witch; who was it you faced?"

My eyes shot up to Dracula's, the memory floating forward.

"Who do you think you are, little witch?" His voice boomed, reverberating through my soul. He was as ancient as I was, but Ambrose looked his age.

I squared my shoulders and looked up into his dark eyes, unafraid when I knew I should be. "Medea." My voice was calm, solid in my confidence.

I watched as Ambrose's face twisted in shock, and then he laughed. "You died in Athens after betraying everyone you loved." My fingers lit with bright orange fire, matching my rage, and I smiled darkly as Ambrose recoiled. "You should not exist."

"No, you are right, I should not, and yet here I am: defending the innocents of this town." It was the first time I acted like a hero, the first time I thought I could redeem myself.

"There is no one to come to your rescue, no one who will stand beside you. This town is mine."

I snorted as his assertion fell on deaf ears, and Kide roared above me, a black outline against a blacker sky.

The Colchian Dragon landed beside me, and my heart soared for all of five seconds before I realized what this meant. Kide had given up his apprenticeship with Hephaestus. And then, to my shock, the lame god, as Vulcan, burst forth in a pillar of flame. The heat that radiated off him was immense, and if I had been anyone else, I would have died from it.

"My lord Vulcan," I spoke with a bow, showing both my respect and my gratitude. He grunted at me, and I knew I upset him.

I flinched and turned back to Ambrose and saw the shock in his eyes. "So, you have friends?"

I shook my head and sighed. "I have a family, Ambrose. I am sorry I had to end yours, but they were making themselves known to the mortals. You can not just wipe out a town for food. Or for fun." He just stared at me. "Leave, Ambrose; I do not wish for a fight, even if the dragon and Vulcan had not arrived. I would have won."

Ambrose snarled at me, fangs and claws extended.

"We are not done, Medea. You and I will meet again, and you will not have your family with you." He burst into a mass of bats and took off into the night.

I turned and looked at Kide, the sadness creeping into his eyes now that the threat was gone. I blew it.

The memory faded, and I looked back at Dracula, the threat Ambrose made still waited for me in my future. I kept my ear to the ground for any news of him, but heard nothing. I knew he was still alive; his death would have sent shockwaves through the community.

"Medea, who was it?"

I answered simply, "Your sire, Ambrose."

VII
UNDER THE FORGE

"My... sire..." Dracula's voice grated on my ears, and I saw, quite clearly, his struggle to keep control. In the past, I would have simply held him through it, but now? My frailty, my mortality would be an issue.

"I didn't tell you, because when I first came to you, I didn't know. You never mentioned your sire the entire time we were together. I only pieced it together after the fact."

Cold eyes stared down at me, and I almost backed up to Kide, but part of me knew I had to stand my ground here. I took a step forward to Vlad and placed my hands on his face, pulling it down to my lips. He stiffened for a minute, and then I felt him relax into the kiss.

"Medea..." he muttered softly as his arms wrapped around my back. I knew he would be all right a moment later when his fingers grazed my neck.

"It's ok love, I'm sorry for the shock. If I had known you would freak out, I would have softened the blow. But for now, let us head to the mountain and see Hephaestus. We can sort things out and then move on."

He nodded slightly and kissed my forehead.

"As you wish, Medea. I am curious to meet him." Vlad slipped his hand around my waist, and we looked at Kide.

"Are you ready, Kide?" I asked softly, looking up at my dearest friend.

Kide nodded and sighed. "I suppose we should get this over with." It was a quiet walk through town, my arm around Drac's waist and my other hand entwined in Kide's. I am sure we looked quite odd as we made our way through the streets of Adrano. Red sun-baked roof tiles of the houses in town lined the tiny roads that had seen countless foot travellers over the centuries. Wagon tracks were ground into the cobblestone from thousands of wheels, and I had to step carefully to avoid rolling my ankle. Aetna loomed before us, casting her shadow over the small town, but it was the shadow of doubt in my heart that almost had me turning back. I had faith in Kide. He could overcome any obstacle, but I knew how much pain it caused him to leave Hephaestus' service. How much pain it caused us both.

Once we were at the base of the mountain, Kide guided us through hidden pathways until we approached an enormous iron door. It was gorgeous, black iron, forged in a time gone by. Kide walked up to it slowly. He looked back at me, and I nodded at him before he banged on the door with a fist.

"Who goes there?!" boomed a deep bass. I felt the anger trembling through the ground, and I nearly took off running back down the hill.

Kide's voice was shaky but resonant. "Kidemonos, Medea of Colchis, and Vlad Dracula."

The door swung open almost reluctantly after making us wait until the sun had almost set behind us, with a screech that sent the local ravens into a cawing frenzy, and the lame god appeared in front of us. He must not use this door much anymore. Red hair and beard, crinkled from the fire, looked darker than I remembered, and his shocking green eyes bore into Kide. I saw my dragon suppress a shudder, and I stepped up beside him.

"My Lord Hephaestus, we apologize for the intrusion, but we have come to make amends," I added quickly.

"I believe this is *his* task," Hephaestus commented with a withering stare. He kept his gaze, iron and flame-tinged, right on Kide.

"You are right, Master." Kide bowed gracefully, his old apprenticeship taking over in an instant. "I am here to make amends; however you see fit."

"Bah!" Heph exclaimed before turning on his heel and hobbling back into the mountain. The three of us followed the twenty-foot god through his forge. I examined everything carefully, the instrumentality and tools of his own design that flew around the forge of their own accord. I knew they were machines and likely used artificial intelligence if he had kept up with modern technology. Granted, he probably inspired AI, along with my dear cousin Athena's help, so it would make sense. However, as Kide and I passed, there was a feeling of apprehension around us, where I could feel them watching us.

"My lord, what do you have planned for Kide?" I asked. I knew he heard me even over the forges and all the noise, but he pretended as if he did not acknowledge my words. The god ignored me and when we arrived at his massive desk, he looked sternly at Kide and I. We stood straight, and I felt Drac behind us, giving us his strength.

"You will both clean my forge. Top to bottom." Kide and I stared at each other and then back at Hephaestus. "This will not be easy, Medea, you have no magic, and Kide, you cannot fly." There was an icy glint in his eye and a dark smile upon his lips.

Kide and I looked at each other again and nodded.

"And how long do we have, Master?" I asked, taking on the position that Kide had taken since we were in this together.

"Until it is done. I believe you have already figured out where you are going next, Medea?" I nodded once more: Turkey, to the lair of my old mistress. "Good, she will not be as easy on you as I am being. Now, get to work." Hephaestus disappeared in a dark puff of smoke and left the three of us in the middle of the forge.

I stared at Kide, and the look of astonishment that sat on his face had me wrapping my arms around his waist. "It's ok, my friend, we can do this. I'll find some scrub brushes and we can set to work. You know me, I'm not afraid to get dirty!" I said, laughing through my fear.

"You're right Medea, of course, you are. Some fire may be in order as well, to help lift the grime up." We turned around, surprised that Dracula had been so quiet and found that he wasn't there.

"A little incentive to get you moving faster." Hephaestus's voice boomed around us. When I looked up, I saw Vlad hog-tied and gagged at the very pinnacle of the forge and I nearly screamed. He was dangling over a vat of molten liquid, and I knew that as time dragged on, the ropes would fray slowly. Neither Kide nor I had the speed to save him if he fell.

"Hephaestus," I growled out, digging my nails into my palms. I winced as I felt blood trickle down my hand, and Kide sighed.

"Let's move, Medea, I know how much the vampire means to you, so we cannot let him fall." He changed shape into the dragon I loved, but the scars on his back had tears flowing down my face.

"Oh, Kide..." I muttered as I ran a tender hand over them. He winced away and began spewing flames around the room. I ran to find the largest wire brush I could and began following Kide around, scrubbing every inch of the forge. There were a few spots that were so greasy, the fire was still burning by the time I got to it, so I waited and moved on. Once the fires were out, I attacked. We became a machine, as we had many times in the past, and soon the floors were polished clean. Then we attacked the tables, tools, walls, everything. I had to climb up on Kide's back to work on the ceiling.

"Medea!" Vlad had called out, and I looked over, one strand of rope holding him in place. How much time had passed?

"I'm coming, Vlad!" I cried out, terrified that we wouldn't make it and I would lose him. I couldn't lose him again! The ceiling was difficult to clean, as the stalactites jutted down sharply from the ceiling. We moved carefully through them, taking care to clean and polish every crevice of the surface. As we closed in on Vlad, I heard a snap and looked up just in time to watch him fall.

The scream that erupted from my throat scared even me. I leapt off Kide's back, my arms outstretched to grab Vlad. I had no power to save him, no way to fly or stop myself from falling into the vat with him, but I knew I couldn't continue living without him. He was my soulmate, even more intricately bound to me than Kide was, and I did not want to carry on in a world where Vlad Dracul didn't exist. My arms latched around his waist, and I pulled him towards me, the two of us falling together, screaming until suddenly we weren't. Kide had caught us and rolled out of the way of the hot metal.

All we heard, as the three of us lay in a crumpled mess on the floor, was laughter.

"Haha... good job!" The lame god sounded smug as he reappeared. "Do you know how long you've worked here?" We shook our heads, fury building in me until I feared I would burst. "Two weeks. I waited for you to finish for two weeks and look at this place. It has never looked so good!" The congratulatory tone in his voice set me on edge and I leapt up and smacked him across the face.

"How dare you!" Heph just raised an eyebrow while glowering down at me. The other two men scrambled to their feet, and I could feel them both readying for a fight. "You threatened an innocent! To what? Teach me a lesson?"

"Vladimir Dracul is hardly an innocent, child," Hephaestus smirked.

"HE IS INNOCENT IN THIS!" I screamed and hit him again. Yes, I know... a mortal hitting a god wasn't smart, but I was pissed. "Why?!"

Heph let my rain of abuse last another moment longer before he grabbed my wrists.

"Because you need to learn that there is more to life than your work, than your powers!" I stared up at him, and I had to blink: I saw tears forming in his brilliant emerald eyes.

"Were you trying to teach me that, or yourself?" I asked softly.

Hephaestus dropped my hands and sighed.

"Both. I knew Kide's heart was true, when he abandoned my servitude for you, for love. But you, Medea? You have never sacrificed anything, truly sacrificed something, for love. You ran away, or you punished others. I understand my wife's part in your obsession with Jason, and for that I am sorry. But when your feelings for Vlad became real, you left. And worse, you blamed Kidemonos for it. It was not his fault."

"No, it wasn't. It was mine." I replied, slumping back into Vlad's arms. "I grew afraid. Afraid that what I had with Vlad was real, and that I would inevitably destroy it, like I do with everything else. I had to leave, to protect him. The fact that it was Kide who pointed it out angered me." I looked at my poor dragon and took his hands after he shifted back to human. "I put the blame on him. Cursed him to never return to Vlad's manor, because I couldn't see a time when I would be going without him."

"And now?" The god guided me to my answer.

"Now, I do not wish to be apart from him, either of them, again. If it had been Kide tied up instead of Vlad, I would have done the exact same thing."

I looked up at Hephaestus. "I would give my life for them in an instant. I would trade my soul for theirs to ensure they survived. Is that what you wanted to hear? Medea, the great Sorceress of Colchis, is afraid for the lives of the two men she loves the most."

Hephaestus took me in his arms, shrunk down to my height, and wrapped me in a hug.

"Yes, child. It is a lesson I, too, have learned recently. I am going to find Aphrodite and try to patch things up. Even if our marriage does not survive, I wish to be on speaking terms with her when it ends."

"I wish you luck, Lord Hephaestus." I replied meekly, wanting to ask if we had fulfilled his requirements but I couldn't find the words. When I heard Kide scream out, though, I tore away from the god and ran over to him. I saw blood oozing down his back and touched the area softly. "Your wings?" He nodded, a cheerful smile on his face before he passed out from the pain. "Kide!" I wrapped him in my arms and held him, worried for a moment that I was losing my dragon.

"Worry not, child. Kidemonos is fine. The bleeding will stop in a moment, and he will be back to himself."

I looked at Hephaestus gratefully, still clinging to the shaking dragon. It was one thing to harm me, it was another thing completely to damage my dragon. If I still had my fire, I'd have been fuming at him.

"And Medea?" Vlad asked softly, his voice broken and cracked. Concern for me wasn't the issue here, it was for Kide that I worried about. Vlad's care for me was more than I could bear at the moment.

Hephaestus regarded Vlad carefully, still unsure what to make of the vampire.

"She knows what she must do. This was Kide's only task. The rest is up to her."

I nodded. I knew it. Hekate was my next trip and after that? If I was a betting woman, I would be back in Athens. I sighed as Kide roused slowly.

"Are you alright, Kide? We need to see *her*."

Kide nodded, understanding what I meant. "Much better, Medea. Now, if we are no longer needed here?" Hephaestus shook his head. "Let us retire back to the manor to rest and heal before we return to Turkey. You are going to need every ounce of your strength to face Hekate again."

"I know. This may be the hardest task yet. I don't think I can do it," I replied softly.

"She is expecting you in three days' time, Medea. You know the time; you know the place. The call has already been put out." Hephaestus commented off-hand. I blanched. No... not that, anything but *that*.

Kide stood slowly, and I wrapped my arms around his and Vlad's waists to help steady them, and we made our way out of the forge.

"Goodbye, Master," he said, his voice soft, yet it carried on the wind to Hephaestus' ears.

"Goodbye my child. I hope you know, I am rooting for you both."

With that, we left the sight of the forge and the trail down the mountain seemed shorter than it had two weeks ago.

VIII
A CONVENTION OF
WITCHES

Vlad booked us a flight to Milas-Bodrum Airport for the second day, which meant we would arrive in Lagina in good time before the full moon. Hekate, Goddess of Witches, Magic and the Crossroads, my patron and the woman who raised me when my own mother couldn't be bothered anymore, stood waiting for us on the tarmac as we deplaned. Her aged face caught me by surprise. I almost ran to hug her, but the anger she radiated had me frozen.

"You are back, child." I nodded, my palm sweating in Drac's hand. "And you bring company with you." She didn't look at either man while addressing me.

"Yes, my Lady. I brought Kidemonos, the Colchian Dragon and my partner, and Vladimir Dracul, the–"

"The vampire, yes I know." Her lip curled in a sneer. My lady had never had a fondness for vampires before, and I had a sneaking suspicion she wasn't about to start now. "And one that can walk in the daylight as well. This does not bode well for mankind, Medea."

The hurt in her voice as she used my name broke my heart. "Vlad does not hunt humans anymore, he does not turn them," I said quickly, knowing that if he were to say the wrong thing, she would destroy him in an instant.

"No, he feeds on you." I blanched and felt Vlad bristle as she turned her gaze to him. "You disgust me, Medea. Look how far you have fallen. If you truly wish to appease me... leave him. Now."

I froze, my eyes widening in fear. I hadn't expected this. But I stood my ground, and I felt my back go rigid as I stared her down.

"I can't. Yes, he feeds on me, and I permit it." The glare Hekate shot my way sent fire wriggling down my spine; I nearly crumbled under her stare, but I remained resolute, shaking the pain away. I had never disappointed her before, but there is always a first time for everything. "You have literally feasted on a piece of my heart, my Lady..."

"I am not your lady anymore, Medea!" she screamed, a maelstrom of black fire erupting from her hands. The wave of flame spread out maybe ten-no, twenty feet around her. The black tarmac beneath us began to melt under the force of her rage. It looked like the sun touching down. It looked like my family's fire.

Even though I watched in horror as my mentor looked to burn the place down, I remained upright and resolute in my determination. The disappointment I felt, I knew, would dissipate in time, but it didn't mean I could not loathe her current display of anger.

"As you wish, Hekate." I looked into the burning onyx eyes that stared down at me. "You can hear the truth in my words. You can feel the truth in my heart. I will *never* send Dracula away from me again. Where I go, he goes, and vice versa."

"You heard the prophecy. He will send you to Tartarus!"

I winced at the pain–the fear?–in her voice. I couldn't identify why that was there.

"Or he will accompany me. Prophecies are always unclear until after the fact. You taught me that."

Hekate smirked. "I am glad to see you remembered *some* of my lessons."

"I remember them all," I sighed, already emotionally worn out from the shock of her anger and her dismissal of me.

Hekate smirked and then looked at Kide and Vlad.

"I will put you three up in quarters near my temple. Tonight, and to-morrow, I will need to borrow my failed student for coven business."

I winced, then threw a questioning look her way.

"The coven is here? All of them?" I shook, trembled, and looked between her and Vlad and Kide.

"Oh yes, child." Her smile grew dark. "Every witch of note from around the world will be gathered for the Hunt tomorrow, so I asked them to come a day early. They will see what has become of the great Medea." With that, she vanished, a cackle in her wake as I collapsed to the ground.

"Oh no, take me away from here... there is no way I can face every powerful witch in the world tonight!" I cried out and turned to get back onto the plane.

"Medea, no!" Kide called out and held me.

"Let me go, Kide! Baba Yaga was one thing. The others?! I will be hu-miliated, tortured! You know this. You know *them*!" I pulled hard against him as Vlad looked on, confused.

"Medea, you know we won't let that happen," he explained calmly.

"You won't be there; you can't be there!" I sobbed, my hands covering my face. "No men, period." I pulled myself out of Kide's arms and ran to the waiting car. We had already given the driver his directions, so when Kide and Vlad entered the car behind me, he left the airport at a rather slow roll.

Outside of the sounds of wind whipping against the windows, silence reigned throughout the ride to Lagina. I couldn't bring myself to voice my fears, and the men didn't want to bother me. There was a small hotel near the temple ruins, one mostly used by the coven, in which we had reserved a suite. As soon as we checked in, they showed the three of us to our suite.

Hekate had gifted us the grandest of the rooms–as irony, I suppose. This was normally the room I would have used as her first and oldest student. As one seeking her guidance now, I should have been further down the rung of power. I threw my suitcase on the bed and ran for the shower. Part of me wanted comfort, but I was still too afraid, too hyped up by my emotions to adequately communicate what I needed.

As I turned the water on and crawled in, I heard the door open behind me. "Not now, Vlad, please," I murmured, almost crying.

"It's not Vlad, Meds, it's me." Kide, of course, it was. "I know why you fear going. All these women, who looked up to you, who feared you, who wanted to *be* you... will see you as weak and mortal. And you're afraid that you'll lose your standing among them." I sat in the shower while the water fell over me, sobbing. "It's alright Medea, I get it."

He did something that he had never done before and crawled into the shower with me. I didn't turn to look at him, but he sat behind me and just wrapped me in his arms. "Medea, whatever the outcome of tonight, and tomorrow's hunt, you will still have Vlad, and me." There was something in his voice I recognized but had never heard from him.

"I know that," I replied softly, leaning against him. It was the most intimate thing we had ever done, considering I had spent the last few thousand years with him. "Why now, Kide?" I asked, worried that I read him wrong and jumped to a conclusion in my exhausted state. It's not like these feelings appeared out of nowhere, but there had always been more of a protective aspect to him than now. Now all I felt from Kide was fear and desire.

"When I saw you dive after Vlad, I knew you would have done the same for me even before you said it. I thought I would lose you. I couldn't bear that. Medea, you have been my world for centuries. Even when we took other lovers. I know how much your soul is interconnected with Vlad. I feel it, too. He is in me as much as you. But when I nearly lost you, I realized that I had never expressed this before, and I couldn't let you die without knowing."

"But," I started, but Kide's fingers rested over my lips as his head leaned down on my shoulder.

"I know Medea, I'm too late. I've had a lifetime and more with you, but your heart belongs to Vlad. I accept that, more than you know and feel how much you two were made for each other. I just wanted you to know." His arms pulled me against him one last time before he started to stand. I turned around quickly and knocked us over.

"Kide stop!" I called out, looking down at him.

Vlad burst into the bathroom, presumably hearing our fall, and just smirked down at us. "Is it finally happening?" He asked playfully as he sat down on the counter.

I raised an eyebrow. "You knew?"

"Of course, I did. Kide wasn't jealous back then, but he couldn't be near us. He hurt. I get that. He wants you, Medea, just as I want you. The question is, what do *you* want?"

The question rang in my heart as a bell tolled in my head. "I want to survive this night," I replied simply. Even I felt the unanswered question of this love triangle hanging beneath me, and I tried not to look down at Kide's body while I hovered over him. I slowly stood up and sighed as he stood as well. I knew his body as well as I knew my own. Could I really give into that? We were one being, most of the time. Would that not make things different between us? I climbed out of the shower and dried off quickly, leaving them in the bathroom. Someone had carefully placed my ritual dress on the bed, and I slid it on. Black lace with nothing beneath it, barely enough to cover myself, with a sheer black fabric connecting the pieces together.

A moment later, after some conversation, Vlad and Kide exited the bathroom and immediately stopped. Kide had seen me in this a thousand times before, but now... with everything that had just come to light? It was as if he saw it, saw me, for the first time. He moved quickly and wrapped his arms around me, pulling me into a rough first kiss. I gasped, unsure of what to do. Should I stop it? Did I want it to stop? What about Vlad? What was he thinking? One look at him, though, told me everything. He was enjoying it. I returned the kiss, something I had wanted in the back of my mind for ages, but then Kide pulled away.

"I know the call has been made," his hand rested on my heart and sighed, "or I promise, tonight would fare differently for you." I blushed and nodded before he let me go, and I walked over to Vlad.

"You didn't stop him?" I asked as he pulled me into a hug.

"And I'm not going to. We have much to discuss tomorrow before this hunt."

I raised my eyebrow, but he simply kissed me with all his heart, and I melted. I could not be this fortunate. Something was about to go terribly wrong. I stepped out of his arms and towards the door. As I opened it and looked back, the faces of the men I loved were happy, and I tried to convey that back to them as I walked through the portal Hekate had set up waiting for me.

When I arrived, I did not land in my normal position beside Hekate at her right hand. That place was empty. I was in the center of the ruin, with the entire coven staring down at me. I could feel their anger and resentment, but I stood there, in the center, like the witch I used to be.

"Medea," Hekate called out. "I have summoned you before this coven to answer for your crimes."

I nodded, still afraid, but I wouldn't let that show.

"The favored daughter finally fell from grace." I heard Arai call out. She was one witch I contended with most, but I heard Baba Yaga shush her.

"Fell from grace, and from power," I spoke, my old air of authority ringing out. "I come before this coven as our Lady has said, to answer for my crimes, but also to seek your forgiveness." I felt the crowd bristle, but I ignored the murmurs and continued. "Any one of you could slay me now if Hekate permitted it. If that is her will, I will gladly accept it." I watched as Hekate's face softened for a moment. "I am mortal and have no power, no gifts, no fire." I kneeled in the ruins, placing my forehead on the ground in front of me. "I accept whatever punishment my lady sees fit. She may no longer accept me as her daughter, but she has always been my mother. Her word is my law."

"Her word is my law," the coven intoned.

Hekate looked down at me and smiled softly.

"What crimes do you admit to? I need to know that you understand what you did."

I had been expecting this, and I braced myself not only for my admissions, but for the cruel strikes, verbal and magical, to come. I felt my shoulders stiffen until their aches rattled my joints.

"Aside from the infanticide and fratricide you all know about,"–the coven nodded; this would have been more recent–"I tarnished the sacred hunt by setting up one for the kill. It was not his time, but I chose it to be. I allowed you all to savor in his murder when I did not take part myself. His fate was not in my hands. I put it on yours. That man was Jason." I heard a gasp roll through the crowd. I don't think they realized who he was.

"He is not dead, oh no. For long ago I cursed him, set him to live for eternity, dying and being reborn, never to father children, never to fall in love. We just happened to meet again, this time, and the anger came roaring back. I gave him to the hunt when he should have been resting in Hades for millennia." I stood back up and looked at Hekate. "He is in Athens, isn't he?"

"Yes, my child, he is. And if you pass this test, he will be your next trial. But first, daughters of mine, what say you?" The goddess of witches called out to her coven. The resounding answer was simple enough. I was to be given to the hunt tomorrow at the next full moon.

The Wylde Hunt would hunt me.

IX
UNDER THE FULL
MOON ON THE
WYLDE HUNT

I had twenty-four hours to prepare. Twenty-four hours until I died. I knew there was no way out of the Hunt. You were caught and then killed. That was it. The Hunt would reap your soul and bring you into the afterlife. I needed to figure out how to survive, but nothing—not one idea came to me. When Hekate had released me from the coven, I raced back to the hotel and slammed the door shut behind me. Vlad and Kide just stared at me. I think they believed I would be away for longer than I was.

To be honest, so did I.

"You're back early," Vlad said, as I flung myself into his arms. Strength wrapped around me, and I buried my face in his chest, trying to keep his aroma in my mind. Emotions flooded me, rising like the tide with the moon full, and a storm raging along the coasts.

I reached out to Kide, who stepped up beside us, and I looked up at him, my voice barely scratching out. "She is giving me to the Hunt."

The pressure from Kide's hand squeezed mine, and I winced slightly. "She can't. You'll die." I nodded. "She gave you no way out?" I shook my head, and he erupted. "FUCK! I'm going to talk to her. She knows better than that!"

"No!" I screamed and wrapped myself around him, stopping him. Vlad's hands rested on my shoulders. "What do you think she'd do if you did? What punishment would she come up with then?! I came here to make my amends, and if that is what Hekate demands, I will abide by it. I just need to figure out how to make it through the night. It would help if I could speak to Cernunnos, but he won't likely show until just before the Hunt."

Vlad placed a soft kiss on my forehead as I pulled back from them and sat on the bed. "Will someone explain to me why we can't just leave? Why must Medea go on this Hunt?"

I bit my lip and shook. Kide sighed and knelt in front of me. "The Wylde Hunt," he explained, "Cernunnos' sacred ride through the realm with the fae and witches to gather up the dead souls and bring them to the Afterlife, was normally an honour when Medea would take part. As a powerful witch, she was a boon for the ride. But once in a while, a mortal would stumble into the Hunt, a live one. This meant one of two things: one, they were about to die, or two, they were to be a feast. Either they offered their soul or their body to the Hunt. The only way a mortal could escape was to plead with Cernunnos. Medea, you have nothing to offer him."

I sighed. I knew that wasn't exactly true. There was one thing I could offer him, but I didn't know if he would accept it or not. I would have to wait until tomorrow night.

"I'll cross that bridge tomorrow. But for tonight... what was it you two wanted to discuss?"

A soft growl escaped Vlad's lips, and I looked at him. "You want to talk about that now, dressed like that?" I hadn't changed out of my ritual dress yet.

"I could change if you would prefer?" I asked slyly. Vlad pulled out a pale purple set of silk pyjamas and tossed them to me. I took them laughing and made my way into the bathroom. The change was quick, and when I returned, Vlad and Kide were sitting on the bed. "So..." I commented as I sat between them.

The air in the room shifted slightly as I felt both sets of lips on my neck. A shudder rolled through me, and my hands rested on the legs nearest. "Kide wants to taste you," Vlad whispered. The moan fell out of my mouth before I had the chance to stop it. "But first, I need to feed."

I nodded slightly, and Kide nipped at my ear. "I want to watch the pleasure of it roll through your body, Medea," he crooned, one of his hands pulling my face towards his, the other guiding my hair away from my neck.

"Thank you, Kide," Vlad said with a smirk. Once my eyes locked with my dragon's, I felt the sting of Vlad's fangs, the rush of his venom, and the sweet release of the feed.

I licked my lips as Kide watched my body shake from the orgiastic nature of the feed. My legs clenched together as I felt a ripple pass through me. Vlad licked the wound closed after disengaging his fangs, and I nearly collapsed back onto the bed. As it was, I had two muscular arms behind me.

"Medea," Kide moaned. Our eyes had never left each other. "Let me taste you. Please?" He breathed, our lips inches apart. I nodded. I couldn't speak. Kide slid off the bed and knelt before me again, and Vlad eased us so that he was further back on the bed, and I was in between his legs. Kide took care, running soft hands up my thighs and carefully pulling down my bottoms. As my wet pussy hit the air, I heard my men breathe deeply. Vlad's arms wrapped around my body and gently eased us back into more of a reclined position, while Kide stared hungrily at me.

"What?" I whimpered; the anticipation was killing me.

Kide smiled then and took a long lick up my slit. "Delicious," he said before moving faster than I had ever known him to and thrusting his 10-inch cock into me. I howled and leaned my head back against Vlad's shoulder.

"Holy fuck!" My body clenched around him. Kide didn't even have to move, and I was about ready to break.

"I have faith, Medea, that you will survive tomorrow, but in case you didn't..." he let it trail off as he slowly began moving inside me.

"I know, Kide. I want this, too." My hands snaked up to his face, and I brought our lips together in a kiss, deeper than before, with a promise that this wouldn't be our last night together.

"Welcome ladies, fae, honoured guest..." Cernunnos had begun his opening address, with a knowing glance in my direction. I stood in the center of the ruins again, wearing a soft green dress and leather boots. "Tonight will be a little different, as we have an *intentional* mortal prey to hunt." I repressed the shiver of fear threatening to escape; I stood back straight, staring at the Horned God. "Here is the deal. Medea has two hours to run, to find somewhere you all won't find her..." there was a collective moan, but all I felt was relief. "During that time, the Hunt *must* take place. You cannot abandon your duties simply to hunt Medea. If I find anyone who has broken this rule, *I* will deal with you, personally."

I felt Arai's eyes on me from behind, and I knew she would come for me, one way or the other. I only hoped that I found somewhere her sight couldn't follow. The good news is, I remembered all of my sister's weaknesses. Arai had a crippling fear of running water. It didn't matter how small the stream was, she could not go near it. The bad part was, none of the coven had the same weakness. Hiding from one would put me in someone else's playground.

I sighed softly as the air crackled with magic. It felt different, ominous, and I wondered if this was what Jason felt before I set the Hunt on him. Poetic justice, I suppose. A bell tolled, signaling the start of the Hunt and I bolted. The forest grew closer, and I ran for it with as much speed as my mortal legs had within them. Once I felt the trees surround me in their embrace, I heard the cackles of the witches and the fae as they took to the air. Two hours to run, two hours to hide... two hours until I died.

Burbling brought me out of my fears, and I darted left towards the river. It wasn't a wide river, but it was deep. I could hide from Arai down there if I needed to, but there were a few of my sisters who excelled at water magic. I only hoped that they weren't so keen on ending me as Arai was. The second bell tolled... I had wasted an hour running already, and the river was nowhere in sight. When I finally caught sight of it, I pushed every ounce of energy into my legs to make it there before the toll of the third bell. It wasn't until I ran into something very large, very solid, and very male before I realized I was fucked, and not in the way I enjoyed.

"Lord Cernunnos!" I gasped, falling back onto my ass. "What are you doing?" I didn't know what I hoped for. I had wanted to speak with him for sure, but not by him materializing in front of me before I could reach some form of safety.

The calculated look in his eyes told me he knew exactly how long I had before the bell. "Why... didn't you want to speak with me, child?"

"I did." I tried catching my breath, but everything about him disarmed his prey, whether it was for food, or for fun. I stood, my knees shaking, and took a step back like a deer, frozen by the primal need to survive.

"Then, speak." When the Horned God gave a command, even the most dominant personality obeyed.

"I would ask for your help to survive this night." I blurted out. He crooked a finger at me and my body reacted without thought, moving towards him.

Cernunnos' eyes sparkled with excitement. "Oh, you would? And what exactly are you offering for my protection... to buy my protection with?"

I had been expecting this. "If I survive tonight, make it to the end of my journey *and* regain my powers, I will bear you a child." Something in the night air sent a shiver down my spine. I knew someone watched me at all times on the Hunt, and that my last hour was nearly up. "Don't imagine you haven't thought of the power your bloodline and mine would carry." I watched the Horned God weighing the decision, and I resisted the urge to dance on the balls of my feet. Waiting made me antsy; it always did, and I knew Arai wouldn't be far. "My Lord, please, I need your answer."

I dropped to my knees and lowered my head, begging him for the response. I felt the minutes ticking by in my head, in my heart, and after a low cackle sounded nearby, Lord Cernunnos finally answered me.

"Yes, child, you have my protection. I will reap the benefits of your bargain, Medea... do not forget it." He placed a benedictive hand on my head and I felt warmth spread through me. The Horned God disappeared, and I flung myself into the river. The only sounds of my success were the howls of rage erupting from my sisters in pursuit.

X
HEKATE FLAYS ME ALIVE

I sank into the river, my body a stone drifting to the bed. I didn't worry about breathing. Lord Cernunnos' blessing would protect me – or so I hoped. Above the water rippled Arai's face, and even from my vantage point, I watched as she pointedly weighed her options. Would she confront her fear of the water to find me, or would she leave me in peace? I knew she had no options but to leave, and I knew I would pay for it later.

"I know you're in there Medea, you can't stay down there forever!" Her voice broke through the water before disappearing. True, I couldn't stay down here forever, but I could stay until dawn when the Hunt would be over.

And so, I waited. Meditating wasn't an arduous task for me, but tonight I was so amped up from the hunt that I had difficulty focusing on my inner self. I closed my eyes and concentrated on the sounds of the river surrounding me. Babbling over the smooth stones I rested on, the water churned in small whirlpools before moving on. Fish swam by; some bumped up against me, curious along their travels, but most just passed on without giving me a second glance. It was an interesting sensation, being at one with the water and Her creatures, all the while not having any power over the element.

"Medea..." a soft voice echoed up the river. I blinked my eyes open and stared into the bluest eyes I had ever seen, eyes that looked familiar to me. My mouth opened to speak, but a finger pressed against my lips.

"Hush, child. Cernunnos gave you his protection, but it is better to not test the blessing if you do not need to." I nodded slightly, transfixed by the beauty of the face appearing before me. It was my face... or at least part of my face. I made out the sharp angle of my cheekbones, and the wide eyes I had been praised for as a young adult. The woman who appeared before me looked translucent, taking form from the riverbed and plants nearby.

I mouthed a single word, and she nodded.

"You are a smart one, my precious girl. Yes, I am Perseis, your grandmother. I am sorry we have never met before now. It was not my wish. But know that your grandfather and I love you dearly, and we are both wishing you all the best luck on your journey." I felt a tear fall down my cheek, though how that happened underwater was of no concern to me. I was transfixed by the sight of my dear grandmother. "When you come back to the surface, you will be stronger than ever, sweet girl. Tartarus will change you." I shivered, and Perseis' hand stroked my cheek lovingly, far more tender than my birth mother had ever been. "And I am sorry to say that your trials here in Turkey are far from over. By skirting around the rules of the Hunt, you may have angered more than you helped."

I nodded sadly, still unable to speak. I had expected that. Cheating, even with the Lord of the Hunt's blessing, was never seen as a good thing. But I was desperate to survive. I *needed* to finish this. If not for my sake, then for Kide and Vlad. I owed them far too much.

"Medea, I know you are of the light. Your grandfather's blessing is strong in you but know that you are also of the ocean. Half of you, more than half, if you go by the mortal's understanding of DNA, comes from the sea. You will need to find that power before your last trial. You will need to harness it, to harness *me*."

I had never controlled the sea, nor had any inclination that my powers were tied to it, but she was right. My mother and Perseis were both Oceanids. I should have some form of water magic at my touch.

Perseis pressed her watery forehead to me and for a moment I felt her power, the infinite strength of the oceans, flowing through me. Sun and sea... the lullaby my mother sang to me came back, and I wondered why.

"I sang that to your father, and he taught it to Idyia. He has the ocean in his veins, as do you, but he denied it, kept you from learning your full strength, as Idyia did." I shuddered as Perseis pulled away, even as her strength enclosed my being. "The night is over, child. You can return to the surface safely now. No one will harm you."

I kicked up off the riverbed and breathed deeply once my mouth broke the surface. The first rays of light broke through the canopy in scattered rays of gold, and I looked at my grandmother with unclouded eyes for the first time. "Grandmother," my voice scratched with newfound emotion.

"My Medea, I wish I had gotten to you sooner. I could have taught you so much about your blossoming powers, not that Hekate could not. But you focused on the sunlight, and your *other* skills. If you would have me now, I will teach you about the other half of your heritage." Perseis wrapped me in her arms, and I felt the world melt away. A piece of my soul clicked into place, and I gasped softly, inhaling the brine of her skin.

"I have no power right now, but when it returns," my back straightened with determination, "I will come to find you." A pulse of power flooded my body, and I dropped to my knees.

Perseis simply held me, and I felt more than magic—a different type of magic—flow through me; I felt her love.

"Oh, child, I wish we could wait that long. But you will see for yourself soon enough. Call for me when you need me. I swear I will be there to guide you." She placed a soft kiss upon my brow, and I collapsed forward as I heard the horn signaling the end of the Hunt and the return home. My legs shook as I stood and I took off back towards the ruins where Cernunnos, Hekate, and my sisters awaited me.

"Ah, the Hunted returns!" Cernunnos bellowed from his seat beside Hekate. I strode into the ruins full of false bravado, knowing that if even one of them went against the wishes of Hekate or Cernunnos, I would fall instantly.

I stared up at the pair of them and squared my shoulders. "I survived Lord Cernunnos, Lady Hekate." The air bristled with anger, but the assembled witches kept their tongues.

"How, Medea?" Hekate's voice was surprised but almost glad as well. She didn't want me dead, only punished, and I had escaped it.

I looked between her and Cernunnos and weighed my options. Telling the crowd here how to escape the Hunt wouldn't be dangerous, but if it got into the fae's heads that I was suddenly breeding myself... that might turn problematic. Granted, I had to survive my upcoming trials before that happened.

"I made a deal with Lord Cernunnos," I replied softly.

The goddess of witchcraft, magic incarnate herself, stared at me, and then looked at the Horned God.

"She didn't?"

Cernunnos simply nodded and the howl of rage Hekate let out flung me backwards into a wall. The air expelled from my lungs, and I hobbled to stand before powerful arms held me in place.

"Arai, Serina, hold her. Use whatever power you have to keep Medea from moving."

The pair of them nodded. They turned me, held me against the pillar and suddenly I knew.

I closed my eyes, fearful of the sting, and screamed out when it hit. Fire coursed through my back with each strike, and I couldn't help myself. I screamed, howled, and cried for mercy. This was the most intense pain I had ever felt in my long life, and I knew it wasn't over. Subconsciously, I counted each strike as Hekate's barbed whip tore through my skin. Twenty, forty, fifty.

When I felt her bone, I passed out, all my strength leaving my body. I couldn't keep it up any longer. The last words I heard were my mother's, Idyia's voice, sounding in my memory: *Sun and Sea, Together into Eternity.*

"Arghhhhhhhhhhhhhhh!"

I woke screaming, sweat beading across my body. No, not just sweat; seawater. The aroma of brine was too distinct to be sweat, and I tried opening my eyes. I had no idea where I was.

"Don't Medea, you shouldn't move." Hekate's strained voice sounded beside me, and I breathed a little easier. "Why, why would you do something so foolish as that?"

The chiding came across lovingly, as if she was fond of me again.

"Do what, Lady?" Vlad asked, and that cued me into our location, we must be back in our room.

Kide's laboured breath sounded nearby, and I wondered how he was feeling.

"What did she promise, Hekate?"

I felt Hekate's eyes on me, and I sighed.

"If you do not tell them, I will."

I shook my head.

"I can't; they'll never forgive me." I whimpered, pathetic.

"Fine, then I will," she stated simply. I was in no condition to argue, but I felt her weight shift beside me, and her voice rang out with the clear tones of truth-speaking. "Medea made a deal with Lord Cernunnos. If she survived the night, continues to survive her trials, and returns from Tartarus with her powers intact, she will bear Cernunnos a child."

A glass shattered somewhere I couldn't see and Kide's voice came to me, distant and hurt.

"That promise... was never to be made. Not without me. Medea, we share a body!"

I winced, but still couldn't open my eyes. "You should have told me, warned me... What will the Fates do if you try to give birth again? Medeius was to have been your last!" The hurt in his voice broke my heart and tears stained my cheeks.

"Honestly, it was the only deal Cernunnos would have accepted. He always seeks to procreate with the strongest beings around. And Medea, whether or not she has her powers, is a formidable woman. He has had his eye on her for millennia," Hekate explained.

That caught me by surprise. I didn't think I was that appealing to him.

"I'm sorry, Kide. I had to. If I didn't make the deal, I would have died easily. Arai had me in her sights the entire time," I paused as a collective gasp surrounded me. "What?"

"Medea, I thought you had no powers?" Vlad whispered from somewhere on the other side of the room.

I tried to open my eyes again, but they were caked shut.

"I don't. What's going on?"

Hekate chuckled and then barked out a laugh.

"Well, it appears your other half is waking up. The ocean is no longer dormant within you, dear. If I had known flaying you within an inch of your life is what it would have taken to bring her forward, I'd have done this eons ago."

I felt a ripple of water rush over my back, and I screamed as the saltwater stung across my open wounds. They didn't close, but I felt them grow cleansed by the pure ocean water.

"WHAT THE FUCK?" Pain seared across my back before a cool cloth smothered it. Hekate's hands pressed firmly into my back as the ripple receded. I felt tape bind the covering to my back and my breathing grew easier.

"Ok, dear, you can open your eyes now," Hekate's soft voice whispered in my ear, and I slowly opened my eyes. She must have sealed them shut so that I wouldn't freak out, since I was on the floor in front of a mirror. I flinched; I looked hideous. Kide was beside me, his chest rising slowly, his breath matching mine. Vlad was near the washroom, as far from me as possible. The blood; it had to be. He wanted to save me from himself and his urges.

I tried to sit up, and Hekate helped me slowly. My back moved in one piece. There was no turning, no flexibility, and there wouldn't be for a long time. "Easy now, Medea. Your little saltwater bath began the healing process. I was wondering if *I* had lost my gifts."

"Why are you being kind?" I spat. My tone was bitter, and I didn't mean for it to be. "You whipped me, tore flesh from bone. Why do you care?"

Hekate looked down at me as she stood.

"You are my chosen one, Medea, the one closest to me in power, in scope, in notoriety. The one to succeed me should I ever fall." I stared at her, scared for a moment. "You are a titan, Medea, not a mortal. Your actions have consequences more widespread than you could ever imagine. Everything I have done has been for you. You will see it... eventually."

I coughed as she disappeared in a cloud of smoke, and I wobbled forward.

"Medea," Vlad raced forward, grabbing my arms, and cradling me.

Kide crawled over, sitting up slowly and cradled my face in his hands. My two loves, on either side.

"A child, Medea, and sea powers? Just what happened last night?"

I stared up into his eyes. Dark blue sapphires shone down on me, and I told them everything. "I promise, if I had seen *any* other path, I would have taken it." I placed a hand on my belly, remembering the joy I felt each time I felt life growing within me. "But Hekate was right, a child with Cernunnos was the only bargaining chip I had."

"With modern advances in science, you should be able to offer an egg or two to him, right?" Vlad offered softly. His cool hands ghosted over my back, offering a calming touch to the burning sensation I still felt.

I looked over at him, the vampire who had captured my heart when I thought no one ever could. "No, this is Cernunnos we're talking about. He'll want to do it the proper way."

"And you want to see what he's like," Kide grunted. "I know you, Medea. If nothing else, you'll take him to bed just to see if the hype around him is real."

I laughed and then cried from the pain. My dragon knew me well. "Yes, you're right, my Kide." I held my hand out to him and cringed at the pale hue of my skin. "I'm sorry, for all of this. I wish we could just go back to Vlad's manor and live quietly, the three of us... but part of me is dying, even as this new strength is raging forth. I..." I hadn't given voice to this fear yet, so I took a deep breath and held onto both of my men. "If I do not regain my powers, even if I come out of Tartarus alive, I will not remain so. My death is inevitable if we fail."

XI
GREECE WELCOMES
ME HOME, SORT OF

It took a week of careful ministrations and painful saltwater baths before I felt strong enough to move freely. At least, that's what I told Vlad and Kide. The truth of the fact was, I felt myself growing weaker. Mortality did not agree with four thousand years of bodily damage and trauma, and all of it had finally taken its toll.

Upon closer inspection this morning, I found a bruise on my upper calf in the exact place an arrow pierced me during the first Punic Wars. I hid it under makeup, but I knew that wouldn't fool them for long. Between my link with Kide, and Vlad's sense of smell, one of them was bound to pick up my changing appearance, eventually.

As it was, I had taken to wearing longer clothing. Today was a floor-length denim dress with an off-white blouse beneath it. The shirt was still light enough to allow air movement, but the denim helped keep my legs out of sight.

"Another plain dress, Medea?" Vlad teased, and kissed me softly.

I chuckled softly, trying not to jar my back too much, and sighed. "If you say so, I happen to like dressing like a mortal woman."

Kide's arm snaked around my stomach lightly and my heart fluttered in my chest as he placed a soft kiss on my lips as well. "I think you look beautiful. So, when do we leave?"

I tried to bend over and pick up my bag and gasped, feeling the newly healing wounds on my back begin to open.

"Medea, no!" They both shouted at me. Most women would love to have two gorgeous men fawning over them, but I was old, ancient by most standards, and I valued my independence. I hated this. Vlad picked up my bag with ease, and Kide guided us out of the room. Hekate had a car waiting to take us down to Bodrum, where Vlad had chartered a boat.

We would sail the Aegean, like days of old, and return to Athens that way. I slid into the back seat slowly, trying not to lean against it. I felt Hekate staring at me from across the parking lot, and I waved at her. She smiled sadly and nodded to me before a puff of black smoke appeared where she had once stood.

The men entered the car, sat down beside me, and we were off. We asked the driver to go slowly due to my injured state, so the trip to the harbor took longer than we had originally anticipated, but soon we were there and aboard our yacht. Vlad had spared no expense when he chartered our journey. He knew it would take us a few days to cross the Aegean, and he wanted to make sure we all travelled with both safety in mind as well as in style.

As soon as we left Turkish waters, the sea turned violent. Poseidon, bless him, was not happy about my return to the Greek seas. We planned on sailing straight to Athens, and only moored off the coast of one of the Cyclades islands for the nights, but the Sea God's wrath blew us straight to Mykonos. Vlad eased the yacht into a berth and made his way to the harbormaster to pay for the night's docking. When he returned, Dracula was drenched, and he sealed the door shut.

"Well, someone isn't happy you're home." He chuckled and began stripping.

Kide looked at Vlad with an amused sense of intrigue and hunger. I nudged him from my seat on the couch.

The dragon just looked at me and shook his head. "Go... it's not like I can." I whispered to him. Vlad looked at us casually, but the glint in his eye signaled that he was hungry. He had kept from feeding on me while I was healing. Because of the magic of the area, he hadn't felt the need to feed, but now that we were far away from Hekate's temple, I saw the hunger there once more.

Kide kissed the top of my head and walked slowly over to Vlad, shyer than I had ever seen him before. "I know you need to feed, and since we have both agreed that Medea needs to rest, I would like for you to take from me." A small gasp escaped Vlad's lips, even though he did not need to breathe, as the request caught him by surprise.

"Are you sure?"

My dragon nodded quickly and craned his neck ever so slightly. Vlad was on his neck in a moment, fangs piercing the skin and I heard a sharp intake of breath from Kide. His head lolled to the side and his shoulders eased. I hadn't seen him so relaxed in a while. It made me happy. After a moment longer, Vlad disengaged from Kide's neck and licked the wound closed. The Colchian dragon slumped into Vlad's strong arms, and the vampire brought him over to the bed. A shiver rippled over the ancient dragon's skin and I smiled softly as he began snoring.

"How was it?" I asked as Vlad sat down beside me.

I leaned my head on his shoulder, just relaxing in his presence and felt him kiss my forehead.

"There was a power in it I have never tasted before, I could almost feel my old wounds healing."

I looked up at him quickly. "Lift your shirt."

"What, now? Medea, you're in no state for that." Vlad teased, but lifted it regardless. I ran a hand over his familiar chest, down his abs, and looked for one of his more recent scars. He and Kide had sparred a couple of days ago while I was on bed rest, and Vlad took a claw to his side. He scarred over quickly enough, but when I traced where the wound should be, it wasn't there. "What, what is it?" Vlad asked worriedly.

I looked up at him, my eyes shining with concern.

"The wound you got from Kide the other day... it's gone."

The old vampire scrambled and tried to feel the long, jagged scar that the ancient dragon had left behind, but found none, just the smooth alabaster skin I loved to kiss.

"How?" he breathed. I looked down, it wasn't exactly a secret, but Vlad had never known the whereabouts of the Golden Fleece. I lowered my gaze, resting my forehead upon his chest. "Medea, how did a wound that should never have been healed, disappear in the span of a few minutes?"

His fingers rested under my chin and as our eyes met the look of worry was replaced with concern. "I have no secrets from you, you know I guard the remaining pieces of the Golden Fleece." Vlad nodded. "But you've never asked about it, where it is, or in whose possession." I paused and watched as the realization dawned on him, his eyes brightening with each second. "Kide absorbed it, shortly after we fled Greece. The Fleece, we realized, could not exist in a physical form outside of its range of power.

Kide was the—no, *is* the—only pure soul out of the two of us. It could only have bonded to him. I never realized that carrying the Fleece in his body could affect you, or anyone, in this way."

I lowered my eyes; the deck seemed more interesting at the moment.

"Medea, you didn't know, right?" I shook my head, but I should have been aware of it. Kide was always a healing presence, now I knew exactly why. "It's an interesting development, my love, but it doesn't change how I feel about you, or him. But we cannot let that knowledge leave the three of us, or everyone will want to hunt him down. And I can't protect you from all that may harm you and Kide, much to my dismay."

"No, the world can never know, our enemies can never know, not until I am at full strength," I said, straightening my back. I withheld the groan. "I will protect you both, my heart and soul, with everything I have." My voice resounded with a confidence I had not felt in a long time, and certainly not since my fire left. My feet carried me up to the top deck, and with that restored energy giving me buoyancy, I raised my voice into the howling winds.

"Lord Poseidon, you may rage and set your storms upon me, but I *will* make it to Athens to face Jason, and I will make it back to Colchis and into the depths of Tartarus. I WILL BE SUCCESSFUL! I will return to my rightful place as a Titan of Light and the Sea."

Vlad had followed me topside and held my hand as the yacht shook.

"Who do you think you are, sorceress?" The weathered sea god bellowed from beneath us. "We cannot even call you sorceress, can we?"

"No, I am mortal and as such you could kill me right now if you desired" I awaited his response, all as my breath barely escaped my lips, knowing that it would only be a moment of pain.

"I cannot, little Titan. Your grandmother has forbidden any of the younger Pantheon from harming you. But this does not mean I will make your journey easy. It is normally a day's sail from Mykonos to Piraeus... Let us just see how long it will take now."

I blinked as Poseidon's voice faded into a watery whisper. She had? She had forbidden harm to come to me? I turned to look at Dracula. His face had grown soft with affection, but his lips only brought passion when they met mine.

"You continue to amaze me, *bella amore*," he whispered into our kiss. I couldn't help but melt into him. "You stare down gods and bargain with ancient primordial forces. You seek power not to make yourself stronger, but to defend those you love." Vlad kept kissing me as he spoke, his hunger not quite abated. "I am so glad that you are back in my life, whatever life throws at us, know that I will forever remain at your side."

My hands snaked up into his hair and I smiled up at him. "And you'll always have me. I am going to fight to survive. You know this." Our lips met, more tender than before and I smiled. "Now, take me down to the cabin and show me what lies in our future. Just be gentle."

The vampire chuckled as he picked me up and padded softly down to the cabin, waking Kide up from his slumber to join in our love-making.

XII
ATHENS ISN'T WHAT
I REMEMBER

I hadn't stepped off the yacht while we were in Mykonos, so the first time my feet hit Greek soil was when we debarked in Piraeus. Poseidon's battering storms had added two extra days to the journey. And in the split second I stepped off, I felt the Earth tremble under my sandals. The stone beneath my feet cracked violently, sending me to my knees. Rock met bone with a heavy thud, and my eyes slammed shut as the pain hurtled through me.

A snarl escaped my lips as the wounds on my back shook before Vlad and Kide could help me up. A string of expletives shot from my lips, surprising the men beside me, and shocking the patrons on the pier.

Scowls from the Athenians greeted us as we trundled up the ancient thoroughfare into the city proper. The ground continued to splinter under my feet as we walked over to a taxi stand and requested the driver take us to The Pinnacle Athens with all due haste.

Once we were safely at the hotel, the tremors stopped and the three of us breathed easier.

"That's better," Vlad commented softly, as he closed the door behind us. I heard the lock engage with a soft *snick*.

I nodded in agreement as Kide put our bags away.

"Where to, Medea?" Kide asked, twitching slightly.

My eyebrow cocked at his movements. "Kide?" He glanced at me and kissed my forehead. "Jason will be where I saw him last."

Kide froze and nodded.

"That's what I feared. The power there hasn't declined in the last two-thousand years, Medea," he warned, "and if Jason has been coming back, being reborn... he may have powers you don't expect."

"I know Kide, I know. Athena's strength is beyond measure there, and I am glad that I've not offended her before," I replied with a soft laugh.

Vlad sighed. "I'm glad there is at least one god you haven't angered, my love, but isn't Poseidon's temple here as well?"

I nodded and shivered.

"And it's on the Acropolis too," Kide said ducking into the bathroom and running the bath.

"Do I need to?" I asked pathetically. These saltwater baths sped up the healing of my back, sure, but the pain of using power entirely unfamiliar to me was almost as painful.

"Yes, and don't argue with me, Medea," he snorted back. "Your grandmother said you'd need this power, and since it's the only one you have manifested, you will do everything you can to master it."

I snarled at him, unconvinced, and closed the door behind them, shutting them both out. "Stay out. I'll do this alone." I slipped into the bath quickly and closed my eyes, concentrating on the ocean in my veins. The water bubbled around me and I smelled the brine filling the bathroom.

Once it felt right, a measure I grew comfortable feeling, I slid my back all the way into the tub. I tried not to cry, but a tear or two still fell down my cheek as I settled down. My breathing shortened as the salt began cleaning the wounds and continued the healing process.

Twenty minutes later, when my toes had turned pruny, I drained the tub and wrapped myself in a fluffy white towel. The wounds from the lashes had stopped bleeding finally, and I looked at them in the mirror. Normally, I had no problems with my body being marked with scars, but these I knew would never fully heal. They would glow silver for the rest of my life, showing my failure.

It should have bothered me, yet even though the scars made me sad, I understood their purpose. I needed humbling, and Hekate had done that for me. I had made a name for myself as bloodthirsty, cruel, and fierce, I didn't need anyone or anything to help me achieve my goals. I believed I had the power to get away with anything, to cheat rules I knew were in place for good reasons, because who could punish me? I was a Titan. My fingers reached around and touched the top tip of one of the scars, and I sighed.

"Medea, are you finished there?" Vlad called in softly.

I exited the bathroom and nodded.

"Did either of you need it?" Both of them shook their heads. "Ok, well, let me get dressed and then we'll head up." I looked out the window and the modern city sprawled out beneath me. I barely saw it, though, my eyes almost peering into the past to see the city as I remembered it.

"Medea..." A voice sounded beside me, one I hadn't heard in millennia.

I turned to look at him and smiled sadly. "Aegeus," my hands reached out to the spectre and watched as they passed through him. "Oh, Aegeus. I am so sorry. What I did to you, you did not deserve."

"Medea ..." he replied again. I knew that would be it. The phantasm was just in my head, my guilt for mistreating the kind king, and for running away from him when my feelings had grown real. And by real, I mean very real; almost as much as I loved Vlad and Kide real.

"Mama..." A second voice sounded, younger than the first by many years, and my heart broke.

Kide turned around to look at the second voice as if he could hear it, too. "Medeius?" he asked, and my eyes widened. He simply nodded.

"Mama, papa," the young boy held out his hands to Kide and me. I fell to my knees and Kide placed a hand on my shoulders. Kide wasn't really Medeius' father, but since we shared a body most of the time, it appears the spirit of my son had felt that connection. The phantasm disappeared, and Kide wrapped his arms around my chest, hugging me tightly.

"That hurt, Medea. Why did he appear to us? I thought this leg was about Jason?" Kide asked. Vlad sat on the enormous bed and stared at us.

I simply shook in Kide's arms. I thought I had gotten over Aegeus and Medeius' deaths, but I suppose not.

"Who are you talking about?" Vlad asked softly.

I looked up at him and whispered my answer. "My third son, and his father. Aegeus was the king of Athens when I fled Korinth from Jason and the murder of my first two sons. I seduced him and he took me in, but I felt for him. I bore him a son, Medeius. But I had to leave Athens quickly when the Erinyes took up my scent. Kide and I ran straight to Asia Minor and Hekate's court when we left. I never knew how their lives changed after I left. I had hoped they would live long lives without my cursed personage there."

"And you're seeing their ghosts?" he asked softly. I nodded, the stain of tears burning down my cheeks. "I'm sorry, you two. This must be difficult for you both."

"It is, yes. We never expected that we'd run into them. Athens should just be about Jason. But there seems to be a mental component here," Kide explained. That was what it seemed to me as well, and I didn't want to admit that it scared me. I hadn't really harmed them, not like I had Jason, and Mermerus and Pheres, but I had still poisoned their lives just by being me. Damn me. Damn me to Hades and the River Styx.

"Regardless," I said softly, wiping the tears away, "if they come again, I will face them, much like I have done every other trial so far."

Kide kissed the top of my head and nodded. "Agreed. Now, let's get you dressed so we can see what your ex-husband wants."

I shuddered and sighed before standing slowly and opening my small bag to pull out a pair of black pants and a light grey tank top. I wanted functionality over fashion today. Something told me I would fight Jason, and I wanted to make sure I was comfortable. Moving was easier now. I tested the scars by stretching slightly, bending left and right. I felt some pulling, but as long as I didn't wrench one way or the other, I should be okay. Or so I hoped.

I felt the repetitive beat in my chest, and I heard the thudding as my blood ran hot inside my inner ears. I wanted to get this meeting over with, and I danced on the balls of my feet lightly. Vlad and Kide just watched me fidget, and I easily detected their own nerves skittering over their skin. I decided it was time. I couldn't wait any longer, and we left without saying a word. The men fell in step beside me, and Kide and I guided the way through the winding streets of modern Athens.

"Welcome, wife," a bitter, disembodied voice boomed around us and caromed off the remaining pillars as soon as my foot hit the remaining Panathenaic Way.

I kept walking. Kide kissed my cheek before peeling off and shooting into the sky like ground-based lightning, if ground-based lightning resembled and sounded like a 20-foot dragon, his squeals filling the dell louder than my damned ex-husband's voice. He would monitor things from above. Even Vlad departed, if only to find a strategic location from which to hide. It was something we had discussed on our extended sea voyage. It left me alone, albeit physically. Their presence remained in my heart and in my mind, and for that I had given thanks.

When I passed through the Propylaea, and looked at the Parthenon *pronaos*, I saw him. Tall as Vlad and as broad as Kide, Jason hadn't physically changed in the eons since I'd cursed him. "Jason," I replied softly, my approach measured.

Jason stepped down and extended his hand. I took it slowly and a bolt of electricity shot through my veins. I nearly doubled over, but I stood my ground. My eyes widened, seemingly of their own accord.

"Dear wife, are you alright?" Jason asked coyly, the tease lingering off the corner of his lips. At one time, his tone and the arch of his eyebrow was enough to melt me and loosen my clothes until they tumbled into a puddle at my feet, but now? I just wanted to punch him.

In the throat.

With a stalagmite.

"I'm fine, Jason. Stop calling me your wife. We are no longer wed. Those vows ended when you died, remember?" I said as a reminder.

Eyes rolled sarcastically in Jason's head as he wrapped his arm around my waist. I suppressed the cringe and wince that should have followed, and he just smiled at me. That perfect smile that captured my heart so many centuries ago.

"Oh, they ended when you murdered our sons," he replied, almost wistfully, as his arms pulled me into a waltz position.

A part of me wanted this, all of this, whether it be reconciliation, blame, or whatever, but I also knew that it was wrong. Jason being here at all was wrong.

"If you want to get technical, you broke our vows when you abandoned me and our boys," I snapped back. Jason's hand tightened around my waist. This time, I winced. His grip turned to iron; if it went any tighter, he would have crushed my hip and several feet of intestine.

"Pain, Medea? Even without your powers, you should be able to handle a little pressure," the voice of my only husband teased at me. "I think I shall enjoy destroying you. Then I shall retake the Golden Fleece, and my curse will be lifted."

A snarl echoed down from the heavens, and I shook my head slightly.

"Don't, Kide, he's not worth your wrath."

Jason looked at me, incredulity dancing in his eyes.

"Kidemonos is not with you?" My silence was answer enough, and he barked out a dark laugh. "This is perfect! I claim this trial to be of combat."

"No!" Kide roared and landed on the top of the Parthenon. "Medea, no!"

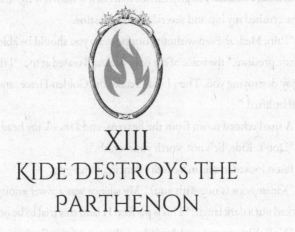

XIII
KIDE DESTROYS THE PARTHENON

Debris scattered around us as Kide's immense claws dug into the remaining roof of the Parthenon. Columns tumbled around us as the ancient monument shook from his rage.

"I forbid it, Medea," he snarled, waves of heat emanating from his maw.

"You *forbid* it?" I hissed, looking up at him. He withered slightly, though he and I both knew that my threat was empty. "Stay back, Kidemonos. I can handle him myself."

Jason smirked, taunting. He picked up a *xiphos* from the ground and tossed it to me.

"You certainly can, Medea." His tone was both sarcastic and teasing. He drew his blade slowly. Without my magic, I was at a disadvantage. Jason was the best sword fighter in all the Mediterranean and had been for years. No amount of curse was going to dampen that skill.

I held the sword carefully, adjusting my grip as I sought a familiar feeling; it had been years since Kide and I had sparred with blades, and I was sorely out of practice. Jason narrowed his eyes at my form, a dark hint of malice pouring from his eyes. I winced slightly, involuntarily. The roof crackled behind me as Kide clawed his way around to monitor me. I knew I had to do this myself, if only to show I wasn't weak.

Jason lunged, a move I knew from decades of watching him; he practically telegraphed it. I parried his *xiphos*, but he countered in an instant. His shoulder crashed against my ribs with something resembling supernatural force. Pain stabbed my side as a gust of air evicted my lungs. I stumbled backwards and fell, landing hard on the marble ground.

"Get up!" Kide howled at me as I struggled to stand.

"Who do you have backing you?" I grunted. My breath was still shallow as I returned to my feet.

Jason glared at me again and smiled, his white teeth flashing between his dark lips. "Does it matter? *I* have power, Medea. You do not."

A scream of disgust erupted from my throat. I charged forward. Jason, my first love, dodged every one of my swings, barely breaking a sweat. I didn't know how long I could hold out. The internal rage felt as if it was about to die off. My hatred and anger for him blew away with the hot Zephyrus winds. I collapsed.

"Medea!" Kide shouted.

I barely heard him before I felt Jason's *xiphos* pierce my chest. It was cold and hot at the same time. My eyes widened from the agony. I opened my mouth to scream, but nothing came forth.

The hot iron tang of blood filled my throat. I coughed as nausea blanketed my stomach. *This is it,* I thought as my eyes blurred with tears. *My end.*

"It is not your time yet, little Titan," a cruel voice whispered in my ear.

"Alekto," I said. My voice was raspy and moist from the blood. Without looking, I recognized her haughty tone. She had chased me for five hundred years. "I thought ... you would be glad to take my soul." Truthfully, I had hoped that it would be Thanatos who came for me. But he only reaped those who died peacefully. This was anything but peaceful.

"Bah! Hades promised me I could ferry you to the Judges when it was your time. This is *not* it!" Her taloned fingers clawed at me, but they passed right through my body. "Trust me Medea, when it *is* your time, I will come for you. But for now, your grandmother has placed certain blessings on you."

I opened my eyes and stared at the Fury. She personified her name. I knew Alekto would relish in my reaping. But I felt my body solidify beneath her hateful glare, and the Erinyes disappeared from my sight.

The brine of ocean air caught my nose as I rolled back to consciousness. My senses returned. Steel clanged against claws in the distance. Cool hands caressed my face. I blinked my eyes to clear my sight. I looked into the distraught face of Vlad Dracula.

"Hey, hey now." I croaked out, reaching up and placing my hand on his face.

His fangs extended in shock. He stared down at me. "Medea?" Vlad's voice cracked with joy. He kissed me deeply. "You fool, why did you fight him alone?" the old vampire asked, after letting me up for air.

I couldn't help but smile. "Because I *have* to."

Vlad looked at me, his face darkening with worry.

"Have to?" he asked.

"Help me stand, please," I said as I began to rise. Vlad helped me. "Thank you." I placed a soft kiss on his lips and picked up my *xiphos*. My movements felt lighter, like my back wasn't torn anymore. "Kide!"

The enormous dragon stopped and stared at me before shifting back into human form. His arms swept me into a tight embrace. Tears splashed down onto my shoulder. I curled my fingers into his hair, holding my oldest friend. "It's okay, Kide, I'm here. I'm okay, I *promise*."

Blue-black eyes stared at me, hard like sapphires. I quivered under his gaze. "If you ever scare me like that, I will enter the Abyss myself and drag you back," he growled at me.

The ferocity of his declaration sent my heart into overdrive, and I kissed him lovingly.

"You know I'm bound for there, regardless," I muttered, our foreheads pressed together. Kide shook his head wordlessly and our lips met again. "I need to finish this," I whispered, turning away from my partner.

Jason glared at me with crimson eyes. I recognized the power within; hatred, one of Dinlas' aspects. Whether Lord Dinlas had given his strength to Jason, or Jason had simply manifested it naturally over the eons, I didn't know.

My ex-husband lunged at me wildly. I ducked, pushing Kide out of the way.

"How are you still alive?" Jason screamed as I rolled away and raised my *xiphos*. He swung his sword sideways at me. I parried the arc of his blade. A metallic ring echoed through the empty Acropolis.

I felt a presence beside me, one I had first experienced in a river in Turkey.

"Medea, it is time," my grandmother whispered in my ear. A cool hand rested on my shoulder. I felt a sudden surge of oceanic power coursing through my veins.

Jason quickly slashed his sword down as if to sever me in half. I lowered my sword and held my free hand up. His *xiphos* passed harmlessly through it and clanged to the floor. Jason's eyes bulged wildly, and I stood straight. "You cannot harm me, Jason. The power of my grandmother flows through my veins. I will deny her strength no longer."

Pushing my hand forward, a jet of water exploded from my palm. It slammed into Jason, throwing him backwards. He landed with a grunt on his back. I walked up to him, holding my *xiphos* out. I pressed the point against his neck.

"This will be the last time I see you, Jason. Whether I get my powers back, *or* I die, I will break your curse. Use your life for good. You owe yourself that."

Keeping the pressure on the blade, I leaned down and pressed my tear-stained lips to his. I pulled away just as I felt his chest heave. "Goodbye, Jason."

I turned and walked away, dropping the *xiphos* to the ground. I stared at the surrounding scenery. Kide's antics had destroyed the remaining Parthenon. I knew I would need to fix it. He remained in human form and wrapped me in his arms once more. I felt Perseis leave me, yet her power—*my* power—remained.

Vlad rushed over and joined the embrace, the two of them bawling at me. Kide enveloped the three of us in his power and we left the Acropolis, teleporting directly back to our hotel room.

Wordlessly, we stripped out of our filthy clothes and made our way into the shower.

The three of us cleaned each other, scrubbing the blood, grime, and dust off our skin. The wound in my chest glowed a dark purple in the fluorescent bathroom light. Once we were clean, Kide picked me up and carried me over to the bed. Vlad was right beside us. Wet lips brushed my neck as Kide sat us down on the bed and I felt Vlad's fangs graze the soft skin there.

My dragon pulled me into his lap, his enormous cock sliding into me effortlessly as if I was made for him. "Ah!" I gasped out, leaning my head back and craning it just to the side, opposite of Vlad's. His fangs sank into my neck at the same time as his cock pierced into my ass. I screamed out and shook between them.

Something clicked within me as if Fate themselves had set something in motion as Kide, Vlad, and I began writhing together on the bed.

Vlad's teeth disengaged from my neck, leaving a dark welt, one I knew wouldn't disappear. A mark, showing his possession of me, and Kide smiled when he saw it.

"Good, my turn," Kide whispered as draconic fangs elongated from his mouth and he clamped down on the other side. The pain was too much to bear, and I exploded, covering both men. I felt them both shudder, goose pimples rising on my skin as their cocks twitched within me. When Kide's lips left my skin, he turned my head, leading my lips to Vlad's.

Our kiss deepened, and Vlad filled my ass with his seed with a groan of pleasure. It was amazing how much he had to give. As Vlad thrust up into me, he pushed me forward onto Kide, and the dragon shuddered. I took both of their hands in mine, riding them hard, as I waited for Kide's orgasm to build to its peak.

"Medea," he whispered softly, resting his forehead on mine. I looked at him before Kide nodded to Vlad. Both men turned my head so that I was looking at them.

"Marry us," they asked in unison.

I didn't even need to think about my answer before nodding. "Of course, I will," I replied happily. As I did, Kide came so violently, my cervix hurt afterwards. His orgasm spilled out of my womb like an ocean wave and I fell forward on him. Vlad wrapped his arms around us, placing a soft kiss on Kide's lips before kissing above his mark. Kide's lips met my skin, and I felt a jolt of electricity race through our bodies, giving my men their second wind.

XIV
COLCHIS IN RUINS

The following day dawned bright and beautiful, a stark contrast to the darkness I felt in my heart. We were nearing the end of the quest, and I could feel my life ebbing away, even as the oceans within roared to power. After Vlad, Kide, and I showered again, we left the *Pinnacle Athens* and made our way down to the Piraeus. Our walk to the harbour was easy. The cracks in the ancient stone vanished over the course of the night. That didn't diminish the weariness I felt. Kide had an arm around my waist, steadying me as sheer exhaustion had control over my body. None of the old men who scurried about the docks stopped us, though we received plenty of looks telling me they recognized us from our haphazard entrance yesterday.

Our thirty-five-foot yacht was waiting, moored where we left her, and we hurried to our departure. We could see the dust cloud from the clean-up all the way down at the harbour and the three of us wanted to be well clear of Athens by the time the claw marks became visible. The news this morning had the Athenian police department out looking for the "despicable being who destroyed their beloved national monument", and we didn't want to stick around for that.

Once onboard, Kide, Vlad, and I made our way topside, and Vlad resumed his place at the helm. He guided us quickly back out into the Aegean without a glance at the carnage we left behind. That was the story of my life until now. Never looking back at my mistakes until it was too late.

The sea was glass smooth, and we expected a little turbulence from Poseidon. I was glad to find that either he didn't care about hindering our journey anymore... or he decided that our next destination was bad enough. That's what concerned me. I didn't know where we were going. I had a feeling that it might be back home, but I had received no confirmation of that. A chill breeze rippled around me, bringing a scent of warmth with it: caraway, berberis and just a hint of ajika surrounded me, filling me with an immediate sense of home.

"Vlad," my voice was soft, far away almost, and he looked at me with worry in his eyes, "take me home, please."

The old vampire simply nodded as Kide sat down beside me. "Are you sure you want to go back? You know who awaits you there."

All I could do was nod and lean against my dragon. My throat dried up at the idea of facing them again, and I curled my legs under me as we began the long journey back to Colchis.

The journey to Colchis was far more uneventful than the last time I took that route. Skylla and Charybdis were long dead, although the sheer rock wall and the bore remained. The Clashing Rocks had settled over the last couple of thousand years as well, so we made the trip in excellent time. Vlad docked the yacht in the port town of Poti and we rented a town car to take us the rest of the way into Kutaisi, what was once the capital of Colchis, Aea. It had been nearly 3,500 years since Kide and I were last here, and so much had changed.

Like Athens, the old city was ever-present, poking through in the weirdest of places. But the ruins of my home broke my heart. I didn't think I cared so much for the old palace, the gardens and the fountains I once played in. My sister's voice rang through the fog of time and I could see her luscious black curls cascading behind her as she ran. I looked up at Kide, at the tears welling in his eyes, and sighed sadly. He was seeing his past too; I was sure of it. We made our way through the dark city. We arrived after dark, and snuck into the archaeological site when no one was watching.

"Kide, look," I whispered as we neared the gates to his garden. The black iron was burnt so badly that I could almost feel the heat from the fire now.

"Who could have done it?" Vlad asked softly, as we edged our way into the garden.

Kide and I looked at each other. "Aeëtes," I replied simply.

As if speaking his name summoned him from whatever plane he now resided in, my father materialised in front of us. Blinded by the light before us, I fell to my knees, screaming in pain.

"Pathetic," cold words in contrast to the warm light assaulted my ears. Aeëtes kept some of his divine glory shining through, and as a mortal, I wasn't equipped to handle it.

"Aeëtes, enough, you are killing her!" I barely heard Kide's screech through the force of Aeëtes' will bearing down on me.

"Enough!" A voice boomed out, one I felt more than heard. Aeëtes ceased his barrage of deific power on me, and reined his light back in. Once he looked like a normal man, albeit an eight-foot tall normal man, Vlad and Kide were at my side. At least, I assumed it was them beside me. Liquid trickled down my cheek. I reached up touching the base of my ear and felt a sticky substance.

"Medea," Vlad's voice came to me in broken pieces, "your ears are bleeding." I turned my head towards the sound of his voice and opened my eyes. There was a fuzzy blob beside me, with what I assumed was black hair, leaning toward me. "Come on, love, get up." I knew his voice, I knew it was Vlad, but I couldn't *see* him.

"Vlad?" I squeaked out and he clasped my hand.

"I'm here love, I'm here." His voice sounded beside me. Someone else took my other hand, Kide, I knew in an instant.

"Idyia," I heard my father's measured voice, "why did you stop me? Our foolish daughter thought it would be a smart idea to return to the site of her first crime." His words were lashes against my ears, and I whimpered, clinging to the men beside me.

"Because she is mortal," my mother spoke softly, in a loving tone I'd only heard once or twice before directed at me, "and because your mother forbade it."

I squeezed my eyes closed and focused on the ocean within. It had healed my lash wounds on my back, and I hoped that it would heal my eyes. I couldn't remain blind. The cool breeze of the Black Sea wafted up towards me and I smiled a little. The now familiar presence of Perseis came with it, and her soft voice echoed in my ear.

"No one else can see me, child, now concentrate. This will sting, and you want to try to keep your screaming to a minimum. My abhorrent son hopes you are blind and thus weakened. He does not know that you have the sea at your command." I closed my eyes further, bracing for the pain. I wrapped my fingers into Kide and Vlad's hands and squeezed as I focused the salt water in my body to surround my eye sockets. I felt each grain of salt, miniscule as they are, passing around the sclera and filtering through the retina.

To say that it burned would be an understatement. I knew fire, and this was far beyond what I could have handled in the past. The saltwater seared around and through my eyes, healing the damage my father's light had caused. It took every ounce of my strength not to scream. I would not give Aeëtes the satisfaction of my weakness anymore.

My hands unclenched as the water receded from my eyes and I stood slowly. Kide and Vlad were naturally at my side, and I was amazed at how well I knew them, their hands, the way they breathed, or didn't in Vlad's case. In the short period of time we'd all been together, their essences matched my own. At least to me, it felt like we were one. I held their love, support, and strength in my hands as I turned to face my father. No, he was never a father to me. I faced Aeëtes and opened my eyes, dark amethysts glaring up at him.

"How are you...?" His voice trailed off as the spectral figure of his mother coalesced behind me. "You are protecting her?" For a titan of light, Aeëtes' voice was ice.

"As your wife, my sister, stated, Medea needs to finish her quest, and I am making sure she gets there." My heart swelled at the love and protection in my grandmother's voice, and I felt her hand on my shoulder. I wasn't alone. In this battle, this reconciliation, I wouldn't be alone.

"As Hera was Jason's patron," I cringed, the past hurt, especially in this place where I could see my life happening around me, "I am Medea's. This is beyond you and me, son. You know who she is to become when she succeeds."

"*If* she succeeds," Aeëtes growled. "She needs to pass me, and *I* do not forgive her for the murder of Absyrtus."

I gulped, *that's* what this came down to. Not that I betrayed his trust, not that I stole the Golden Fleece and ran away with a Greek "hero". No, it was all about my little brother.

"Nor should you." I commented, my voice soft, almost delicate. Aeëtes looked at me, hatred flowing out of his golden eyes in sparks of fire. "I murdered that little weasel in cold blood, and given the opportunity, I would do it again." The men let go of my hands, and I felt their eyes on me. Neither of them knew, and it was time I told Aeëtes the truth.

"Your conniving, manipulative, abusive little brat raped Chal, repeatedly when we were children." Aeëtes and Idyia's eyes widened visibly, and the light dimmed around the titan.

"You didn't know? Of course, you didn't. I hid her as best I could, whenever he was in a state. She nearly bore him a child, until your sister stepped in. One of the nicest things Kirke has ever done was save Chalkiope the embarrassment of bearing our brother's spawn." The light faded and Aeëtes shrunk back down to his normal human height, his power diminishing.

"You could be lying, to save your skin," he muttered, nearly inaudible over the wails Idyia began spewing. I simply rolled my eyes at her; I didn't have time for her drama.

"I could be, or you could summon them." My reply was simple even though my heart was racing. Chal was my world, until Jason. Protecting my baby sister was everything, and I needed the truth to be known.

Aeëtes recoiled from the suggestion and shook his head before looking at his mother. "Is it true, Mother? Did I raise a monster?" Idyia crumpled at her husband's feet and sobbed. The ocean in me stirred with her distress and I almost reached out a comforting hand to her.

"Aeëtes, Chalkiope was your light, your hope, and you let your pride get the better of you." Perseis was right. Even as children, I knew the path I would take, the Fleece had shown me some of my future. Absyrtus' tendencies showed themselves early and I wasn't always around to stop him.

"Medea knew, when she left with Jason, that she could not leave Chalkiope unprotected. The decision was cold and calculated, and absolutely correct. You would not have a kingdom if Absyrtus had been left to inherit it."

That more than anything I said withered Aeëtes. The great son of Helios fell to the ground and shook, the rubble scattering away from the force of his pain.

"Colchis survived as long as it did, father, because of what I did." Aeëtes raised his head in protest, but I held up my hand. "No, I didn't know what would happen to the kingdom, or to you and mother. All I knew was that Chalkiope, my beloved, precious, flower of a sister, would never be mistreated at the hands of someone who should have protected her. That is a decision I will never regret."

I knelt before him and placed a quivering hand on his knee and felt the shuddering cease slowly. When our eyes met, I saw my reflection in his golden eyes, I looked just like him. I was always my father's daughter. "My regret, Aeëtes, is not telling you sooner. Maybe I could have fixed it, or maybe I would have made it worse. But for hiding the truth, I am sorry."

I bowed my head in deferential respect and closed my eyes. Something was telling me this was important, and I learned centuries ago to trust my instincts. Time passed, inconsequential to the scope of what my parents had to come to terms with, but after waiting what seemed like hours, two hands rested upon my head. One was cold, the deepest part of the ocean in it, and the other burned, the forest of the sun radiating down into me.

The wind swirled tempestuously around the three of us as my parents laid a benediction on me. I couldn't understand what they were saying, but the feeling of final acceptance, of love, of reconciliation was one I had never known from them. It encased me, flowed through me and part of my heart healed, a part that I never knew was broken. Tears streamed freely down my face as Aeëtes lifted my chin.

"Rise, daughter, you have passed your test." His voice was serene, beyond calm, and it made me wonder what just happened. "You now have the strength you need to finish your quest, but there is one thing left to do."

"What?" I croaked out, my voice pretending that it couldn't speak.

Idyia pointed at the tree, the tree that once held the pride and joy of Colchis. It was the tree that Kide used to curl around and protect. As he followed my eyes our jaws dropped and my heart broke. "You must heal her."

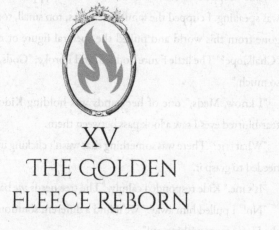

XV
THE GOLDEN
FLEECE REBORN

I stood slowly, my legs moving of their own accord, and Kide joined me. Vlad hung back, but I felt his heart with us, so it was ok. We made our way, hand in hand, over to the tree. Blackened bark, withered limbs, she had certainly seen better days. I reached out to her, feeling the pain she went through over the years since our departure, and I cried. Kide wrapped me in his arms, and I felt his despair splash down on my head.

"How did we let it come to this?" He asked me, his voice barely above a whisper.

"I don't know, love, but I promise we'll fix it." Kide's hand rested about mine and I sighed, leaning against him. "I don't know *how* to fix you, old friend."

"She needs the Fleece." A pale whisper appeared from within the tree. "*We* need the Fleece."

Kide dropped his hand from mine as a face appeared where the voice was speaking. I cupped the familiar features, too small, too precious to be gone from this world and pulled the spectral figure of my sister to me. "Chalkiope?" The little figure nodded, and I broke. "Gods, I've missed you so much."

"I know, Meds," one of her hands was holding Kide's and through tear-blurred eyes I saw a look pass between them.

"What is it?" There was something that wasn't clicking in my brain, I just needed to grasp it.

"It's me." Kide responded calmly. "The tree needs *me* back."

"No!" I pulled him away. "We'll find a different solution; we can extract the Fleece from within you!"

"That won't work, Medea, and you know why." Chalkiope spoke calmly. She always knew how to manage my rage.

I pulled away from them both, anger building in my chest. "I refuse to give you up. I can't... Kide... NO!" My body curled on itself as I screamed out, and I wrapped my arms around myself. "I can't lose you; I can't lose you."

Strong arms wrapped around me, and I leaned back into my dragon. "I will always be with you, Medea. My soul belongs to you, it always has. But the tree needs me, more than you do."

"Do you think I could have made it this far orsurvived as long as I have without you?" Kide simply hung his head. "Do you think I will survive Tartarus without you?"

His head snapped up and crimson eyes stared down at me before I felt the surge of his power surrounding me. A moment later the great beast who dominated this landscape stood before me, his great wingspan shielding me from all eyes and encircling the tree.

"Do *not* do that to me, Medea!" I winced; the force of his voice sent shivers across my skin. A moment later, the man I loved stood before me, yet his wings remained around us as if disembodied. Kide's hands cupped my face, and he brought my lips to his. "I love you Medea, with every fibre of my being. I need to know that you will continue this fight without me."

His lips met mine and I melted into the love we shared, into our history. Kide's hands lifted me up as he sat down, and he placed me gently on his lap. "I can't promise that, Kide, you know I can't." I pressed my forehead against his and sighed.

"My beautiful sorceress," I scoffed darkly before he growled. My body shuddered at the sound, and I looked up at him. "You are, whether you have your powers or not, you are still my beautiful sorceress. You've already gained some power you never knew you had, and now?" His agate eyes scanned my face and he smiled. "You inherited it, you know that?"

I cocked my head to the side curiously. "Inherited what?"

"The position your father held. Aeëtes is no longer a titan of light, *you* are. You are Helios' heir." I stared at him, my mouth hanging open.

"No, I can't have. I don't have my powers back." I protested. Kide's hands slid up my shirt and I moaned softly. "Kide... Here?"

"Here, Medea," he growled so deep I felt the reverberations in my own chest. "Look in the mirror, when you return to Vlad, it will tell you I'm right."

I couldn't tease out what he meant because Kide pulled my shirt over my head. As he dropped it on the ground, Kide's lips claimed mine, and I melted. My hands travelled along Kide's chest, unbuttoning his shirt as I went. I pulled it off quickly, not realizing just how much I needed him right now.

"Slowly Medea, slowly." He whispered, lips grazing my ear and tugging on my earlobe gently.

"I can't go slow, Kidemonos, I need you. I need one more time with you before I give you up." I couldn't stand the begging in my voice, but it did the trick. My lover hiked my skirt up as he broke the zipper of his khakis with his immediate erection. We shuffled a little to slide them down and expose his full length for a breath of a second. Once he was fully free, Kidemonos, my dragon, my dragon and soul-bonded partner sheathed himself within me. I held back the scream as ten inches of delicious cock pierced into my body.

"Kide..." I whimpered softly and rocked against him. I needed every inch; I craved the feel of him coating the insides of my womb with his seed.

"Shh woman, just..." he grunted possessively, "let me love you." I nodded and leaned my head against his. We sat there, our bodies one and writhed together slowly. There was need, desire, a craving neither one of us could escape, but love most importantly. Always love. I would carry a part of him with me forever now.

My toes curled slowly, and I began to shake, I was so close. I looked up at my first friend, my constant companion and nodded once, a simple gesture to convey a lifetime of love and he pulled me back into a kiss, the deepest kiss I had ever known.

"I'm there, my Kidemonos," I breathed into him.

"Me too, my Medea, together?" He asked, hands curling into mine.

"As we always have been," I replied, kissing him again before I broke. My legs shot forward, straightening before my toes curled again and my orgasm splashed down Kide's thick cock. I screamed, I couldn't help it, the ecstasy was too much. But then I felt his cock twitch and knew his last load would be his biggest.

"MEDEA!" Kide roared, a stream of blue fire erupting from his mouth, he aimed up and away. As he came, his wings expanded, opening wide and I stared for a moment: they were gold. As Kide continued to pump within me, flecks of gold shot out of his wings, leaving the protection of the dragon they called home and reformed into a single being.

The Golden Ram was reborn, birthed from Kide's orgasm. I nearly laughed, but as he finished, and the Ram took a step forward, I felt whole. There were many instances in this journey where I felt a completion of my soul, and this rocked me to my core. The Ram nudged me with his head, and I reached out a tender hand. The tiny sheep nuzzled me and let out a small 'baa' before he nudged Kide and did the same thing to the great dragon.

Kide pulled in his wings, and we stood up slowly disengaging from one another and redressing. We linked our hands again and walked with the Ram to the tree where he promptly curled up at the base. I felt warmth radiating from the tiny animal and smiled as the magic began. The Ram was beginning to heal the tree. I looked at Kide and leapt happily into his arms.

"You did it! You healed the tree!" I exclaimed, kissing him with the knowledge that he would now resume his place as the guardian of the Fleece.

"No, sister, you both did." Chalkiope's spirit floated over to us and took both of our hands. "You had to be willing to let go of your most prized possession. Not the Fleece within Kidemonos, but your eternal friendship. Kide needed to, well..." she coughed a little embarrassed. "He needed to release the shards that resided within his blood. That could only have happened one way."

"But we've, umm... released before now." Kide commented, flushing a deep red. Aeëtes, Idyia, Perseis and Vlad all rushed over as they saw the tree begin to bloom, scattering soft black petals down on us.

"Yes, but the first condition was not met." She replied. "And do not worry, Kidemonos, it is not you who will be protecting this Ram. *I* will be the one remaining. The tree and I have already bonded over the last few thousand years, I am now the Protector of the Golden Fleece."

I smiled, realization dawning and pulled my semi-solid sister into a hug. "I will come and visit you, I promise."

"Oh, I know you will. Your future here in Aea is far from over, big sister." She replied with a knowing smile. "But for now, you have one last hurdle to overcome. You need to head to the Acheron, to see Charon. He will take you into the underworld."

I suppressed a shudder, even in the summer heat. "I know, but is the Acheron really the best way in?"

"It is your only way in." Chal replied simply. "Any other route will kill you."

Vlad had reached my side and wrapped his arms around my waist, placing a small kiss on my neck. "We won't let that happen."

"No, we won't." Kide asserted with a dark growl. "But if we're heading back to Greece, we should probably leave soon. The trip will be long."

I nodded a little and hugged Chal again. "I love you, sister, I will return here first, when I rise from Tartarus."

"I know, and we will await your return." She replied calmly as my parents and grandmother stood beside her.

"I can offer you no more aid, Medea," Perseis spoke plainly. "You know who you are, you have the strength to achieve your goals, and you have a future to come back to. Now you just need to seize it."

"I will, grandmother." Perseis smiled affectionately at me, and I looked at my parents. They seemed diminished somehow, but happy. For the first time in my life, they smiled at me and made me feel like their daughter. "Be safe." Was all I could say before I turned, my men beside me, and feeling the whoosh of Kide's translocation back to the yacht.

XVI
THE DESCENT INTO HELL

Leaving Colchis this time was much smoother than my original exodus. My parents forgave me, my sister was safe and in fact bonded with the tree that kept the Golden Ram, and I had the love of two men surrounding me. You would think nothing could dampen my spirits, but no. No matter how beautiful the day, how calm the sea, or how gorgeous Vlad and Kide were, I was moody.

You would be too if you were about to travel to the Underworld.

"Medea, just come topside and bask in the sunlight. You'll feel better." Kide called down to me. It had been three days since our departure and I hadn't left the cabin.

"No, thank you, I'm perfectly fine down here." Yep, I was sulking. I didn't care, though. I pulled my legs up to my chest and sighed a moment before the door opened.

"Enough Medea, we're all nervous about this last leg of the trip." Vlad picked me up quickly and threw me over his shoulders.

"Put me down Vlad, now!" I demanded, feeling like a child in his arms. His body shook with laughter, and I bounced on his shoulder. The vampire didn't respond, even as I kept screaming at him like a child.

"Alright, my love, as you wish!" he chortled before tossing me overboard once we reached the top deck. Kide stopped the boat and sighed.

"Now I'll have to go get her." He said playfully and began pulling off his shirt.

"Oh no, she can manipulate the water, remember?" Vlad parried, and Kide stopped. I glared up at them as their momentum carried the boat further from me.

I had never tried to manipulate the sea in this manner, to actually be a sea god, so naturally, I floundered a bit. Perseis wouldn't help me here. This I had to learn on my own. So I closed my eyes. I felt the surrounding water, the cool wind on my face, the blistering sun beating down. My hands spread out under the surface as I searched within me to find some connection to the element beneath me. It took a moment, but as if Perseis was here beside me, guiding me, I felt that push toward the edges of my power. It was a strain I wasn't used to feeling, but I knew I was on the right path. Little whirlpools began gathering at my hands, slowly pushing me towards the boat. I didn't need my eyes open to know that Vlad and Kide were staring at me, watching intently.

The pools grew bigger, pushing me up and out of the Aegean, and I landed on the tilting deck with a flop. I knew leaving whirlpools alone would either increase their size or give them time to die out. I didn't want to wait and see which option they took, so I closed my eyes again and concentrated on calming the waves beneath us. Once the sea settled, I rolled onto my back and looked up at the two men.

"I'm not speaking to either of you." I snarled at them and got up slowly. I went to make my way below decks again but was stopped by a shirtless, tanned dragon who blocked my path with a single raised eyebrow. "What?"

"Enough sulking, Medea. Do you think this journey is easy for Vlad or me? Do you think I want to watch you head into the underworld? You're mortal now, for gods' sakes. The moment your feet cross the Acheron, fuck, the moment you board Charon's boat, you will begin to wither. Do you really think we haven't been thinking about this too?" By the end of his tirade, Kide was screaming.

"I'm sorry," I replied simply, and wrapped my arms around him. Kide's arms wound around my back, and he held me tight. "I know, you're right. I'm being childish."

"You are," he chuckled, "but that can only be expected from one as young as you." I smacked his chest playfully. Kide was maybe a thousand years older than me? We never really did the maths, but he was a "teenager" while I was growing up in Colchis, so it was better *not* to ask. "Remember your promise to Mermerus and Pheres." I blanched.

"You're right again, I swore I would see them again." My back stiffened, and I kissed Kide's smooth chest. "Alright, on to Epirus." The men simply laughed as Vlad took over the helm and we cruised around the Peloponnese.

Three days later, the yacht cruised into her final berth of the trip, a dock in the small town of Parga. We paid the docking fee, took care of the rental, and stayed in a hotel overnight. We would make the rest of the journey on foot because the entrance to the Underworld was not on GPS.

Walking through Athens was one thing, while I could feel the age of the city, the polis, with every step I took, these backwoods in the Epirus region were still wild. The mountain ranges on the Peloponnese were still under Pan's domain, and if I was being honest, normally I would be looking for any sign of the randy satyr, but now? With two men and the promise of a future tryst with Cernunnos? I'd never wanted him to stay away more!

As the Ionian Sea faded into the background, we climbed through the wilderness heading upstream of the modern 'up-world' Acheron. The vegetation here looked withered, decayed almost, like being close to the river sapped their lifeforce. The Acheron was the River of Woe after all. It made sense that plants and animals would lose the will to live if they remained.

Even though we were still in the land of the living, I could feel the misery building in me, soaking up through the soles of my leather boots and creeping into my soul.

"Why are we doing this again?" I muttered despondently, more to myself than the others. "I could just curl up and die here."

Kide had taken to the skies, lucky bastard, and he called down to Vlad and I.

"I can see the spring, I'll land in a moment, but you're almost there."

Normally his voice would have given me hope, but not now. We weren't even on the banks of the proper Acheron and I wanted to turn back. The only things that kept me going were my sons. Seeing their faces again after all these years was my hope, my guiding light. It wasn't my powers, or this new position as the Titan of Light. I hadn't taken the time to look in the mirror as Kide had instructed me to in Colchis, I didn't want to see the truth, and he hadn't pushed. But to see Mermerus and Pheres again, kept most of the misery and woe away. I just hoped it would be enough once we were in the Underworld and on the Acheron itself.

The bubbling of the spring sounded softly in my ear and I could almost hear the cries of anguish coming from below it. The cave entrance was nearby. Kide and I had been here once before while escorting Hekate on her pilgrimage back down, but we had never passed the threshold. As Kide landed and shifted back to human form, the cave came into sight. Dark and foreboding, the black obsidian walls gleamed as menacing mirrors, taunting and twisting our features into ghoulish versions of ourselves.

I shivered, the warm summer air did nothing to warm me as we neared the cave entrance. Vlad and Kide's hands wrapped into mine and we entered the cave to the Underworld. Ten steps into the cave, the floor fell out beneath us and we plummeted straight down. I knew it was the way in, but with everything going on, I had completely forgotten.

"KIDE! Transform!" I screamed as my fingers scraped against the black walls. I found no purchase, no finger holds to grab onto.

"I can't, it's blocking me!" He replied shouting over the whooshing of the air around us.

"Same, my powers are blocked." Vlad added. I knew there was something at the bottom, and I was hoping my suspicions were correct. A moment later I heard a splash, then another and then I was submerged into frigid water, fighting to come up for air.

This was not sea water, and I would have no control here. If Vlad and Kide had been unable to use their powers, I certainly wouldn't. As my head broke free of the surface, I gasped for air and quickly took in my surroundings. There was a ledge a few feet away, and a tunnel leading further down into the earth. The descent into hell indeed. We swam quickly for the ledge and pulled ourselves out of the water. I lay back on the smooth, cold surface and blinked my eyes open, clearing the water from them.

"Are you two alright?" I asked, coughing and looking for them.

"Ya," they both replied at the same time. We took a few more breaths then rose to our feet, and looked down the path. Kide found a torch and lit it with a burst of blue flame, and as the tunnel illuminated, those ghoulish caricatures we saw of ourselves on the surface were even more grotesque down here.

The hands linked together and we continued our way into the Underworld. As we walked, the sound of wails drowned out that of the river, and I knew we were close. Vlad and Kide wrapped their arms around my back to keep my shivers at bay, but all I heard were the voices assaulting my ears, those of the men, women, monsters and the two children I had wronged and killed during my lifetime.

"Don't listen Medea, focus on the feeling of Mermerus and Pheres in your heart, and you'll overcome this." Kide whispered to me. I nodded slightly and we continued down the path.

The tunnel opened up into a giant cavern, where the souls of the dead waited at the side of a pale blue river. A skeletal boat was docked at the bank, and on the top stood a broad shouldered, dark haired gentleman. I walked up slowly and he turned to look at me. Where eyes should have been were two obsidian black orbs, glaring back at me.

"Medea, you and your companion are not dead. You cannot cross." Charon's voice grated out slowly. He didn't need to use it often, but when he did, he always made it seem like such an inconvenience. "The young one is dead, he may board, so long as he has payment."

Vlad looked startled. He always had such life, full of vigour, that I often forgot he was the undead.

"Charon, we come bearing drachmae," Kide stepped forward, a large bag appearing in his hand. Charon's gaze shifted to the dragon and he smiled. Crooked and greedy, Charon's smile looked out of place, another thing he rarely did.

"This will buy you safe passage for three into and out of the Underworld. None think this far ahead."

"We did, we have a future to get back to and I wasn't leaving anything to chance." Kide replied. The psychopomp held out his bony hand and took the coin purse from Kide before allowing us passage.

"When we return, whatever is left over, I would like to buy the passage for as many souls as you can, please. The rules have changed and people are not buried with drachmae or possessions anymore to cover the fare." The request was a simple one, but I knew it was important. The souls of those who don't have the funds to get across should not be left in limbo. They deserve the same rights.

"If you survive the journey, we shall see. Regardless, I shall bring it up with Lord Hades at the next meeting." Charon replied slowly.

I nodded and boarded quickly. As soon as my feet hit the deck, I crumpled. The wails of the dead struck me violently. The boat tilted as they sensed living souls above and Charon had to fight to steer it straight down the Acheron. Kide and Vlad hovered beside me as I clutched my ears trying to keep the sound out. I knew it wouldn't work, the wailing was in my heart.

I have no idea how long we sailed down the river, but once the Phlegethon and Cocytus joined the Acheron, my screams joined the chorus of wails coming from below me.

I heard a cackling sound from behind me and turned slowly, my body shaking violently from the effort and I looked up at Charon. His face was split in a hideous grin and his voice joined the others.

Medea, look how far you have fallen... Medea, finally eating that piece of humble pie... Medea, brought low by her own past, her own children...

My sobs racked my body. I couldn't look at the men, Charon's obsidian gaze bore into my soul. When I finally decided to end it and began moving to throw myself overboard, the boat stopped and Kide lifted me effortlessly before stepping onto the dock.

My back straightened, I stood up still in his arms, and Vlad joined us.

"I will wait for you here, little titan, but maybe you will not need me." Charon jeered as the men dragged me away from the shore, and away from one despair, only to be greeted by another.

The great gates of Hades stood before us. Taller than Hephaestus' at Aetna, but just as magnificently crafted, the black marble shone in the torchlight. Two human sized handles made of obsidian almost beckoned us forward, but I stood fast. I looked at the men.

"Whatever happens in there," I felt them both bristle, ready to jump in and correct me, but I stopped them, "*whatever* happens, know that I love you more than my own life, and I would not change one minute of our time together." Before they had the chance to respond I stepped forward, and opened the gates to Hades' kingdom.

XVII
UNTO THE GATES
OF HADES

The great marble doors opened before us, and I gazed into Hades' kingdom. Acrid sulfur assaulted my nose, you would think I'd be used to it by now, living with a dragon for the last few millennia, but no. This was far more potent than Kide's breath. We took a cautious step into the kingdom and heard a soft growl emanate from nearby.

"Cerberus," I muttered. Why didn't I think to bring something to appease the giant three-headed dog? Because I thought I'd be long dead by now.

"I'll keep him distracted," Kide said as the ground shook beneath our feet. The guardian approached, but Kide transformed back into his dragon form and roared fiercely, a stream of blue fire erupting from his maw. *Now, Vlad, take Medea and run!*

Dracula picked me up effortlessly and ran at his full speed towards the palace. Behind us the barks and growls of Cerberus clashed with the roars from Kide. Eventually he would have to take flight to get away. I hoped he would be safe.

"Ok Vlad, you can put me down now!" I shouted over the whistling wind as he ran. Vlad skidded to a halt and set me down, just inside the palace gates. I wheeled around just as Kide took to the skies and heard the angry barks turn to sad whimpers as Cerberus' prey got away. We would need a plan to get past him when we left.

A few moments later, after dodging some harpies, Kide landed in human form and I threw my arms around him.

"Don't do that again, please. You scared me to death, Kide." I kissed him softly as the dragon wrapped his arms around my waist for a peaceful moment. Vlad coughed and I wheeled on him. "And you, next time you decide to follow his orders, don't. Or at least, warn me, please." I slapped Vlad's chest but he just laughed at me.

"Yes honey, now should we continue? Do you know where you're supposed to go from here?"

I only had two clues, Tartarus and my boys. I turned my head, just to the left, where I felt a cold wind blow. I didn't want to pass the Judges, they would absolutely take this opportunity to find a way to keep me here.

"This way," I said calmly. I knew it had to be Tartarus first, there was no way I could face my sons without passing through that final test, and I wanted it to be on my terms, not because of some prophecy.

Vlad and Kide looked at each other, then at me, and fell into step beside me as we began the slow walk around Hades' palace. Secretly, I hoped to see the God of the Underworld, or at least Persephone. I had always had good interactions with them before. But if this leg of the trip had fewer gods in it,

I would be happy with that too. They weren't too forgiving with the living being down here, so my plan was to avoid them and pass through the Fields of Asphodel.

The Fields were a boring location, if truth be told, it was where most souls ended up. Those who just lived, so didn't stand out in any way were sent there. It was something of a wide open plain of sadness. The good thing is that most souls don't retain any form of consciousness after their judgement, so they don't even realise where they are.

"Medea!" A deep voice boomed out through the palace grounds. I froze, not wanting to see my great-grandfather.

"Is that ... ?" Kide whispered, leaning down. I nodded and turned very slowly in the direction of the voice.

"Lord Hyperion," I sputtered, bowing slowly. I would never forget the lashes in the ground beside me when my manners failed. And that was when I had the power to *attempt* to defend myself.

"Oh, come now, child, I believe we are well beyond that now. Hyperion will do nicely." He replied as he sauntered up to us. His dark toned skin blended in with the atmosphere of the Underworld, but I didn't know how he could be so removed from the sun all the time. The Lord of the East, of the rising sun always seemed more at home here in the Underworld, whether it was under Titan or Olympian rule.

"Hyperion, what can I do for you?" I asked, the heat he was radiating was making me sweat.

He smiled at me, and I felt sick to my stomach. Something was wrong with his gaze. "You can tell me how you received my grandson's blessing, how I don't sense his power coming from Aeëtes anymore." I stared up at the immense Titan and wondered how to respond. "And who are these two fine gentlemen escorting my favourite great-granddaughter in the Underworld?"

"This is Vlad Dracula," I gestured left. He bowed and extended a polite hand to Hyperion who shook it jovially for a moment before releasing it with a cruel smile. "And you know Kidemonos," Kide took a step forward and bowed as well.

"The Guardian, truly, Medea. You *do* still walk in exclusive circles." He was hinting at something, but I couldn't place what. "And what is this I hear of a deal?" I choked on my spit.

"Which answer did you want first, Hyperion?" I asked as Kide patted my back. Their hands entwined with mine and I felt a little better for their reassurance.

He paused for a moment and brought one of his hands up to stroke a small goatee. His fingers glowed as they touched his skin and the pulse of heat that sparked off him nearly had me stripping. "Aeëtes, start with him, but Medea?" My head snapped up at his command. "I want the truth." I nodded, how could I not?

Between the three of us, we retold the encounter with Aeëtes and Idyia, and then the rebirth of the Golden Ram and Chalkiope's instatement as the new Protector of the Fleece. He nodded along, as if he already knew all of this, but wanted our confirmation.

"And the deal you made?" He prodded, a little more heat emanating from his body. I had to take a step back.

"I promised Cernunnos a child, if I survived the Hunt, and then returned from the underworld." I whispered.

"And why did you offer that? The bloodlines should never mix." His voice was cold, a stark contrast to the natural heat that surrounded him and I jumped at his tone.

"It was all I had to offer to survive. I had no power, Perseis hadn't shown up and gifted me her strength yet, and Aeëtes had not blessed me with his power. I had nothing else. Offering my life wouldn't have done the trick, or I would have just let the Hunt take me."

"And what of your men, I'm sure they would have offered something." He countered. I flushed and looked at Kide and Vlad.

"I would have sacrificed everything to keep Medea from making that decision." Hurt pushed through Kide's voice and I looked over at him. A single tear glistened in his black eyes.

Hyperion nodded. "And you, Lord Vladimir?"

My gaze moved to Vlad and he shook his head. "That is not for your ears. Medea, Kide and I have much to discuss when we return to the surface, but for now, my words are for them alone." Pain was there too. Had I been selfish? They couldn't accompany me on that journey. It was a decision I had to make alone.

"Why are you doing this, Hyperion?" He had never acted particularly familial towards me or my siblings.

"Because dear, your actions have consequences, especially down here. Every move you make, every inch you take towards your goal comes at the cost of something or someone else." I stared up at him. "Have you not realised that yet? Look back over your journey and tell me I'm wrong. Go on, I'll wait."

My hands fell from Kide and Vlad's and I stared at the Titan, my great-grandfather, and desperately wanted to punch him.

"I can't." I whispered, my shoulders low in defeat.

"Because you are selfishly motivated. It's a family trait, little girl. Each of us who bear the gift of light, whether magnificently like your grandfather and I, or as yet to be seen, like you and your sister," my head snapped up again. Chalkiope had never once shown any penchant for having our family's power. It's what made her special.

"Chal doesn't..." I began before Hyperion placed a blistering hot finger on my lips. I recoiled from his touch, almost cold in the heat.

"She will, once the Ram is full-grown, she may even end up more powerful than you, little witch." Loathing dripped from his voice and instinctively I reached for my powers, I knew a threat when I heard one, but they never came. Not the sun fire that I was so accustomed to using anytime. As I reached inwards, the ocean within erupted and a jet of water burst out from my hands, hitting my great-grandfather square in the chest. He stumbled back a few feet, looking at me in surprise.

"The blessing of Perseis, you shouldn't have that power." He growled and began to grow in height and brightness. Kide was in front of me in an instant, his wings expanding and wrapping around Vlad and I, protecting us from the direct power of the sun. The air around us shook, with a gravitational force akin to a small star and we were flung back towards Hyperion before he released that power and we were shot into the air. I knew that power, Supernova he had called it once, while berating my form on fire whips. He told me I'd never be able to use it, let alone withstand it if he were to unleash his full potential. Now I understood why.

As we soared through the sky, I tried to get to Kide. He took a direct hit from the blast, and I needed to know if he was ok. Vlad held me tight though, until something hit us. One of the harpies, if I had my guess, and Vlad let me go. I lost him as we fell, my arms and legs flailing, wishing I had some of my old power back. It was a futile wish. As Kide rolled in the sky I saw his back: charred black, he looked like asphalt. I had done this to him, *I* brought him here. If it wasn't for me, he would be safe and alive. I choked back the tears that threatened to escape. The ground was rushing up at us and I still had no idea where Vlad was. A mass of bats approached as I neared the ground and swarmed around me, slowing my descent.

"No, Vlad, Kide... PLEASE!" I shouted, worried that Kide was dead, or dying. I needed Vlad to worry about the dragon, if I died so be it. I watched the ground near and tried angling myself to lessen the impact, but I knew that this was going to hurt.

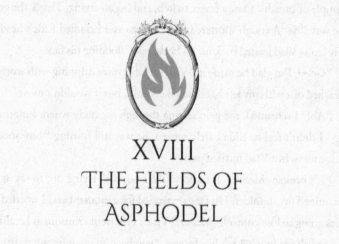

XVIII
THE FIELDS OF ASPHODEL

CRACK! I landed on my left shoulder moments before the unconscious mass of Kidemonos landed and crumpled beside me. I crawled over to him as Vlad settled back down as a man and rushed over.

"Medea! Kide! What happened?" He asked frantically as he rolled Kide over onto his back. "I need you over here, Medea," he whispered, realising that Kide wasn't breathing, and Vlad couldn't help with that. I continued my hobbling over and fell beside Kide's head.

"You'll need to do the compressions, Vlad, I can't," my voice was hoarse, and I indicated my arm. Vlad nodded and began the compressions, moving deeper and faster than he would have for a regular human. When he nodded, I took a deep breath and pushed the air into Kide's lungs. I didn't feel any resistance so nothing was blocking his esophagus, which relieved me. My next worry was for any broken bones from the fall, but I knew he was tough to break.

"Come back to me, Kide, please," I whispered before giving him another couple of breaths. I saw a finger twitch, and began crying. Thank the gods he was alive. A cough sputtered from his lips and I cradled Kide's head in my lap as Vlad leaned back on his heels, relief flooding his face.

"Good, I'm glad he made it." Vlad said, his voice dripping with worry. I reached out with my left hand, to take Vlad's, but it wouldn't move.

"Ah!" I screamed, the pain searing through my body where a moment ago I didn't feel it. Kide barely moved, he was still rousing from unconsciousness, but Vlad hurried over.

"It's broken, Medea." He said softly. I nodded, trying not to cry as he examined my shoulder. His fangs extended for a moment and I worried he was going to lose control. "Medea," Vlad's eyes went crimson, as I realized he hadn't fed in what felt like forever, "you have an open fracture, there is blood. I can't..." he stopped and took off. I looked around, trying to see where he went, but there was nothing in the gloom.

"Vlad!" I shrieked out, scared of what could have happened to him. I couldn't leave Kide though, not in this state. He began to mumble softly, and I knew he was coming out of it, but I was still worried. Beads of sweat formed on Kide's brow and I used my good hand to wipe them away. I could feel a fever raging in him, and wished that I could help. I leaned forward, placing a soft kiss on his lips and cried for the first time.

"Medea..." he croaked out and I looked at him, leaning forward quickly.

"I'm here, Kide, you're okay. I'm here." I kept stroking his face, grateful that he was speaking again.

"You're bleeding," he coughed and I nodded.

"I'm sure I am. Vlad said I had an open fracture on my left arm, and that my shoulder was broken. It's okay, Kide, I promise, we just need to get you up and healthy again." I couldn't tell him that I barely felt the pain, because I knew my time was growing close.

"Medea!" Vlad called out as he came racing back, with help.

I looked up at the newcomer and shook my head. "How did you find him?" I asked, startled.

Vlad just smiled softly and shrugged. "He found me, he even had this with him." Vlad held up a blood bag and I sighed. "He seemed to know we were coming."

"Yes well, his father is the god of Prophecy. Hello Asklepius, it's been a while." I turned to the original mortal doctor before his ascension and smiled. "Can you help him?" I indicated to Kide, barely breathing, but slowly showing signs of life.

"I can, Medea, but first I need to look at your arm." I pulled away as he stepped forward. "Come now, you are no child, Kide has already begun healing his internal wounds, I *need* to look at that arm. If I do not heal it now, I will be removing it in about an hour."

That stunned me into compliance. Asklepius never minced words, but he was always honest. "As the doctor orders." I leaned back, as he took my arm carefully.

"And he does. How far did you fall?" He asked as I felt a warmth begin to spread through my arm and into my chest.

"We were in front of Hades' palace when Hyperion intercepted our travels. He went supernova. I'm sure there are others who need tending? Argh!" I gasped as the bones began resetting.

"Well, you are on the outskirts of Asphodel now, so, you fell pretty damned far. You should thank the vampire. If he did not slow you at the last minute, Medea, it would be your neck that was broken, not your arm."

I looked at Vlad as he gulped down the last of the blood bag. "Thank you, Vlad, for me, and for Kide."

"I couldn't let you die, Medea, either of you. I'll not be the cause of the prophecy in that way." He stated simply. I shuddered as the words returned to my mind.

Love shall be your guide, your soul to rend and mend, beware the abysmal pit, the mirror forth shall send. Asklepius' voice sounded very much like his father's, and I had to look carefully to see if Apollo hadn't switched places with him. "It is closer than you think, Medea, you *will* go to Tartarus, and soon."

I hung my head. "I know."

"Ok, how does that feel?" He asked as the warmth receded. I shrugged a little and winced. "Hmm, perhaps a sling?"

"Nope, I draw the line at looking frail. The outside does *not* need to match the inside." Asklepius laughed and nodded.

"As you wish, now onto Kidemonos." He began to work his magic on Kide, focusing the healing touch on his back and wings, which had taken the brunt of the damage. "He was hit with Supernova? By Hyperion?" I nodded as Vlad knelt beside me and took my hand.

"Your dragon is made of far tougher stuff than I gave him credit for. He will rouse shortly, do not let him use his wings, even to pull them back in. They need to finish healing as is. And just think, if you had waited to release the Ram from within him, he would be perfectly fine by now." I sighed as Asklepius spoke. He pulled back his glowing hands and stood slowly.

Vlad helped me to my feet after placing Kide's head down gently and I bowed respectfully to the young god.

"Thank you, old friend, for saving him," I replied, thoroughly grateful, "both of them."

"Humility, Medea, from you?" I hung my head. "This journey really has changed you."

"I hope for the better." I said, smiling at him. He shook Vlad's hand and turned away.

"Remember, no wings." I nodded before Asklepius disappeared.

We seemed to be safe here for the moment, so Vlad and I let Kide rest. I held Vlad's hand still, but I kept my eyes on Kide's healing back. It worried me that it was taking so long.

After what felt like an excruciatingly long time, Kide woke and rolled to sit up. The growl that rumbled from his lips would normally arouse me, but this time, I just wanted to comfort him. Kide took Vlad and me into his arms, holding us tightly. Vlad let out a gasp of air, which was shocking since he didn't breath. But me? My lungs were crushing under his strength. I tapped Kide's arm slightly and he let go.

"I am so glad you two are safe." Tears flowed freely from his eyes as we pressed our foreheads together. To be alive, or undead, in the Underworld was a blessing we wouldn't take for granted. "Where are we?"

"On the outskirts of the Fields of Asphodel." Vlad replied, placing a soft kiss on Kide's cheek. "We're both relieved that *you* survived. You took a direct hit."

"I know," he said, rolling his shoulders. It was something he did before caching his wings, but Vlad and I hollered at him. "What?"

"Don't use your wings, even to put them away, Kide. Asklepius said not to, and I worry about why. You could lose them altogether. Please, just let them heal." I explained quickly, trying to prevent him from inadvertently using them.

Kide looked between us, we must have looked terribly frightened, because he simply nodded and sighed. "Alright, I won't."

"We'll remind you if you try, my friend." Vlad chuckled softly to lighten the mood. "Onward?" He suggested.

Kide and I nodded as the three of us stood and faced the Fields. "Onward," we replied together.

I mentioned the fields were boring, right? It seemed as though we passed through the entire Underworld before I saw anything that remotely called to me. Spectral figures had surrounded us, milling about as if still living, but totally devoid of intelligence, until one stood out among the rest. He was taller than the ghosts, and wore a long black cloak. Nothing was particularly special about the cloak, but the man's scythe was distinctive. I gestured for the men to hang back, especially Vlad, and took a few steps towards him.

"Hello Thanatos." I called softly to him, my tone of voice slipping from my usual brash to a softer, more polite version.

"Ah, Medea, it is good to see you. Though," he checked a pocket watch that appeared out of thin air, and closed it before it disappeared, "it is not yet time for you to be here."

"I know, I am on a quest." Thanatos hissed at the word. It had been ages since a proper Underworld quest had taken place, and most of the time it was to retrieve something from Thanatos.

"What do you need from me?" He asked, turning his gaze toward me finally. Hollow eyes in a classically handsome face stared down at me, and I lowered my gaze respectfully.

"Nothing, honestly, I am simply passing through, on my way to Tartarus." I replied, knowing full well that he wouldn't believe me.

"That is what they all say, Medea," he scoffed and passed his scythe from one hand to the other. I felt a wave of death pass over me and nearly succumbed to it. As my knees hit the ground, Thanatos looked down at me again. "Speak truthfully child, why are you actually here?"

"I am being honest!" I gasped for air. This wasn't the peaceful death I had been hoping for, but if Thanatos decided it was my time, so be it.

"Then why bother me?" He asked quickly, a seething annoyance in his voice.

I shook my head. "I do not know, this was the path we took and you were here. Why are you here?" The wave let up and I breathed deeply. Vlad and Kide rushed over and Thanatos took a disdainful look at the vampire.

"None of you belong here, leave." He said, turning away from us.

I stood up quickly and reached out with my left hand, wincing at the pain, and grabbed his arm. "Thanatos please! Nothing in this journey has been accidental. Why would someone lead me to you?"

The god of death wrenched his arm out of my grasp lest it kill me and he turned back to me. "I visit here, ok?" I looked up at him, as pale-blue human looking eyes formed where the hollow sockets had been. He was beautiful. "The children, I visit the children that I reaped, too early to be here. I visit them, to make sure that their afterlife is as nice as it can be. Not all children are godlings, or demigods when they die. They are not all the children of kings and queens and can afford passage to Elysian. Some are left to wither here in the Fields of Asphodel until the spirit dissipates. These are the children I visit. These are the children who should have been protected."

I instinctively reached a hand up towards his face, a single tear streamed down the pale cheek, and I knew that my own face was stained by tears as well. Thanatos didn't flinch away, but I didn't touch him, I just held my hand above his face, trying to put as much care and love into it as I could.

"I know you escorted my sons here, Thanatos, I regret what I did beyond measure. Trust me, if I could go back to that moment, I would not repeat those actions. It is truly the only thing in my life that I regret." I looked back at Vlad. As much it hurt to leave him when I did, looking back on it now, it was the correct course of action. But murdering my sons? Never. The anger and jealousy that Aphrodite's curse had inspired in me would forever be my defining moment. Maybe I wouldn't be here now if I had fought the rage, maybe things would be different, but I would save them if I could.

"I know, Medea, did you know they cried for you?" I stared up at him and shook my head. "They were smart boys, they knew you had been cursed. They also knew that you made it painless for them, not to ease the burden on your soul, but because deep down within that love wench's curse, you wanted to spare them pain." My hand fell against his face, and it surprised me with how warm he was. Perhaps Thanatos was the most in touch with the living out of us all. "Go to them, they want to see you, and I know you want to see them."

"I do, but first I–" my words were cut off as talons dug into my shoulders and hauled me away from Thanatos, Kide and Vlad.

"So close to the pit, Medea! And now I get to take you there!" Alekto cackled as she flew us deeper into the Underworld, and closer to Tartarus.

XIX
THE ABYSMAL PIT

I thought about fighting Alekto – in fact, it was one of the first instincts I had – but trying to break free of her talons would have caused more damage than I needed. Plus, once I started to fall, she'd just catch me again. So, I let her take me.

I was bound for Tartarus anyway. I guess this would be my ticket to hell.

"Medea!" Through the maelstrom of Alekto's hair, I saw Kide running as fast as he managed, and Vlad flew just above him. "We're coming!"

"Meet me down there... We all knew this was coming," I called back, unafraid for the first time since Kide and I left Orcas Island.

The men looked at me, stunned. I rolled my eyes and sighed. Idiots.

"Yes, that's right, Medea. You know what awaits you, don't you?" Alekto teased me.

I looked up at the Fury and nodded.

"Yes, I know what my punishment will be. I told you, I have accepted my fate."

"That meddlesome healer shouldn't have fixed your shoulder. I would have enjoyed hearing your screams while I dragged you to your torment. But this, knowing that you *know* what awaits you, it's almost as good. Just one little scream, please?" It came out as if she had almost begged me. I truly didn't have the heart to fight her. She had waited to have me in her talons for almost four thousand years, so I let out an ear-piercing, albeit faux, shriek, just for her.

Who says you can't give your enemies nice things?

"Thank you!" she clapped, almost giddy in her laughter.

"You're welcome, Alekto. Will you take me straight there?" I asked softly, not wanting the men to hear.

"Yes child, I will." Her voice softened to an almost matronly tone, something I would have never expected from her. "I know why you did it, even if I can't forgive you, or her, I understand." I stared up at the Fury, the one who had been my bane for centuries. She always kept tabs on me even after the hunt was called off officially. I saw sad eyes staring down at me.

"We aren't intentionally cruel, Medea. We punish those who have done wrong, egregious wrongs. Wrongs that should never be forgiven. Some, very few, manage to escape their punishment. All deserve it though," Alekto explained.

"I know, and even when I was fighting to survive, I never hated you, or even begrudged you. You serve an important function, all three of you do. I'm sorry I made your years more difficult. Did..." I trailed off. This was it. The spot I had come to, and I felt the freeze of fear settle on my heart and mind. I felt fear – great amounts of primal, blood-curdling fear – in just thinking about inquiring about this... "Did anyone slip past you or your sisters while you were hunting me?" My voice cracked, weak and shaky, and a sulphuric tear hit my face. It sizzled before blowing away, leaving a faint scar.

"Only a couple," she answered; I felt my heart drop an instant later as she continued, "but we managed to find them down here, and meted out the justice necessary."

"I'm sorry. I shouldn't have been so selfish. My life doesn't outweigh anyone else's. I should have known that."

Alekto halted and stared at me, hard, as if parsing my words and dissecting my tone. She nodded, seemingly sure of my answer, before she then turned and flung us into a steep dive.

This time, my scream was about as real as Zeus' body count.

Minutes later – at least that's how it felt; damn that adrenaline rush! – Alekto set me down on the ruins high atop a hill overlooking Tartarus.

"This is ..." I started and she nodded.

"The crest of this hill is the heart of Tartarus. You already relive the pain of murdering your sons, everyday. Your punishment is simple," she said as she picked up two vials, filled to the brim with a black-red liquid I knew to be the blood of Tartarus. "Two vials, every day. Since you are alive, this will be an interesting test to see how long you survive."

I took them both. As soon as they were within my grasp, the faces of Mermerus and Pheres appeared on the warm glass. I expected this. "One for each." I raised them in toast, and drank both vials quickly before collapsing into a writhing mess of shrieking pain.

In my daze and impenetrable stupor, I thought I saw Alekto looking down at me, sadness creeping across her eyes once more before she disappeared.

For the first time in weeks, I was utterly and horribly alone.

Days passed. Maybe weeks. I didn't know: I wasn't keeping track. My body had started the slow decaying process. Soon enough I would turn into a withered, emaciated shell of a human, barely strong enough to lift the vials to my sunken lips, but I would continue. I had to.

I heard crashing outside the ruins and screaming as voices filtered up to me. When I finished the second vial, I fell back to the ground and shrunk even more. I knew deep down what had happened to me - I would slowly become one with Tartarus, the primordial being whose heart I drank from.

"Medea!"

My name; at least, I think that was my name. It sounded unfamiliar, untuned, to my ears.

"Medea!"

There it was again. And the voice, I think I recognized it? Maybe? Possibly.

Gods, I wanted to die.

Someone lifted my head and cradled it. "Oh gods, what have they done to you?" Sympathy dripped from their–his?–voice and I cracked open my eyes.

"Who are... Do I know you?"

My voice didn't sound like mine. It sounded like death, haggard and thick with bonemeal.

"Medea, it's me. It's Kide, your Kidemonos. Please come back to me."

Through unfocused eyes, I saw the face above me, the voice it belonged to, had tears streaking down his beautiful face. I lifted a hand to his skin. It had a warm tinge to it, one that dared me to leave my bare palm lingering too long.

"You are beautiful, has anyone told you that? Hmm... you should leave this place, go find yourself a wife. You are far too perfect to remain here."

My head drooped slightly.

"Kide, just get her and let's go, I can't hold them back much longer." The second voice, or maybe it was the first, called from the door. He seemed familiar, too. Another male.

"No," I said softly.

"No?!" they cried out together, incredulous.

"No," I restated, before my tone turned from that of a funeral march to that of a bloodthirsty snake. "I deserve this, this punishment. Do not take it away from me!" The vials appeared once more, the faces of two beautiful boys shone brightly and I mumbled the only names I remembered. "For you, Mermerus, and you, Pheres."

The one called Kide, who knelt beside me, tried picking me up, but couldn't manage it. I had somehow grown heavier than I looked, and that was thanks to my guilt.

Yes. My guilt weighed me down. That was how it happened here: Tartarus and the vials forced the guilty party to recall all of their crimes, from the heinous one to the very first innocent crime that set one on the path to degradation, and it became the chains that bound one to this primordial plane.

A bright blue jet of fire erupted from his lips, and I struggled to cover my eyes in the dim light.

"No, you promised you would see your sons again, and by the gods I am going to help you keep your oath, Medea!"

He tried lifting me again, but his feet sank deeper into the heart of Tartarus.

"Stop Kide, take Vlad and go." Names of people I once loved danced on my tongue, like I craved them. "Please, just go. All that is here for you is death if you remain, and I can't be responsible for that. Please."

I clutched at Kide as he continued trying to lift me.

"No Medea, we're not leaving without you." Vlad turned to look at me, and his face brought emotions back that I thought I had reconciled. "Right Kide—"

For one long dead, I had never imagined how a vampire would sound or look like when staked. Was there that strangled puff of air emerging from what remained of his lungs? Would blood as black and as thick as tar spring from the wound and from his mouth? Would the vampire, doomed to die again, burst into a thousand million molecules as fine as powder? I had never thought I would see the day.

Well, again, seeing as I had done in many a vampire before. That was eons ago, and that was a memory forgotten, lost to time.

Still, when a bone-edged blade appeared in Vlad's gut, and his words cut off, I soon entered a nightmare even worse than the one I now occupied.

"Vlad!" I shrieked and leapt out of Kide's arms, the first time I moved in uncounted days, outside of my daily victuals. Rage built in my soul, slicing the hold Tartarus held on me, and I clenched my fists, moving around the vampire as blood gurgled to his lips.

Oh Gods, it was as black as I had imagined. I tried to keep that out of my mind as I swung at the demon behind him. A roar from the rear came seconds later.

"Take care of him, Kide," I demanded as I engaged the beastly demon, the one holding the blade. My fist struck the side of its head, below the horn, and it evaporated from the scene. Exhaling sharply, I grabbed the handle and pulled the knife slowly out of my lover and held it expertly in front of me, licking it for a moment. Vlad's blood surged through my body, invigorating me for the moment while I went on the offensive.

The swarm of demons came, maybe twenty or thirty, I didn't count. With precision strikes even in my semi-weakened state, I swung and cut through each and every one of them. Once I had a second blade, I became unstoppable. Bone blades sliced effortlessly through the viscera of demonic flesh and I relished in the screams of Vlad's attackers.

Minutes ticked by, possibly hours, before I finished; the demons vanquished. I turned back to the ruins and saw Vlad leaning up against Kide. The smile that broke across my face, I felt, had the power to illuminate Tartarus for years, if I'd had my powers back. As it was, I leapt into their arms, careful to avoid Vlad's wound and kissed each of them deeply.

"I love you, both of you, but you can't stay," I whispered, surprised at my own voice.

"We came to tell you, neither do you!" Kide said. "We knew you'd decide to stay, your guilt would keep you here even more than your promise to the boys."

I nodded gently.

"Well, we have insurance to guarantee your safe departure from this Abysmal Pit," Vlad commented cockily.

I couldn't help but be intrigued.

"Oh? How?"

Kide pulled a large bottle out and shook it. I worried that he'd made a deal with a djinn, but when smoke slipped through the mouth and took form, I nearly choked.

When Aphrodite appeared, I slapped her.

"Yikes!" she cried out, rubbing her perfectly blushed cheek. "Ok, I suppose I deserved that."

"You deserve a hell of a lot more, bitch," I growled darkly.

"Yes, I know, that is why I am here, silly." I raised my eyebrow at her and she continued, all the while curling a strand of that perfect strawberry blonde hair around her finger, as if she hadn't a care in the world. Ugh, it nauseated me. She really was a skank of the highest order, but there was a part of me that couldn't deny that she's got it going on. "The Three have decreed that you have suffered enough, especially if after this little debacle you tried getting them to leave." She pointed at Kide and Vlad.

"And..." I coaxed, I knew there was more to it.

"And I would be here for the next four thousand years serving your punishment, since I am truly to blame for the death of your sons. You would never have murdered them if I had not intervened, both times."

Wait, what? My eyes bulged, and my breath caught in my throat as my heart skipped a beat.

"Both?" I gasped.

"Oh yes. I made you fall inexplicably in love with Jason; granted, I did not *need* to, seeing as you two had a destiny. But then I intervened when he met Creusa and wed her. So really, all your early problems were *my* fault. So, here I am, going to serve my time."

I nearly hugged her, the newfound surge of life making me think impure thoughts. Instead I held out my hand to shake it and she stared down at me before taking it slowly.

"Thank you, Aphrodite. I," I swallowed and looked up at her ocean blue eyes, "I forgive you." Her eyes widened in surprise. "You were doing what is in your nature. I'm not OK with it, and I wish I had been stronger, but I forgive you."

"So I do not need to serve time?" she asked hopefully.

I just laughed.

"Oh no, if the Three decreed you had to serve, then you shall. But I am going to see my sons before I return to the land of the living, with or without my powers. I believe I've proved to myself that I don't need them.

The powers do not define who I am. I am Medea, daughter of Aeëtes and heir to the Throne of Light."

With that, Kide wrapped Vlad and I in his arms, translocating us effortlessly out of Tartarus.

XX
A FINAL RELEASE

When we emerged from the translocation void, a warm breeze greeted us shortly before four arms wrapped around my waist.

"Mama!" they cried out, and I sank to my knees.

"Mermerus, Pheres!" I cried. I couldn't help it. Kide and Vlad had let go of me in my descent to the ground with my sons, but I knew they weren't far. "Look at you two. You look just as I remember."

They giggled softly.

"Well, of course, Mama," Pheres said, smiling, "We do not age here."

I leaned back and looked at them carefully. There were no spots or blemishes from the poison. Being in the Elysian Fields must be good for their health.

"Mama, you have come so far, in such a short time," Mermerus said, taking one of my hands. He looked so much like Jason that my heart hurt to look at him, but I smiled nonetheless. "Do you know how long you were in Tartarus?"

I shook my head. I didn't really want to think about it. Time made no sense down there. I knew I had to drink two vials a day. Sometimes they seemed closer together, and other times they felt weeks apart.

"No, there was no way to keep track of the days, not really."

"Two years, Mama. You were in Tartarus for two years."

I stared at them both.

"And you call that a short time?" I chuckled, trying to play off the fear I knew Kide and Vlad would have felt during that time.

Pheres took my other hand and brought it up to his cheek. Warmth flooded into me and I smiled at him.

"Considering you have been punishing yourself for 4,000 years? Yes, two years is a very short period of time."

"You are both so wise. Clearly, you got that from your aunts," I laughed, then hugged them as tightly as I could again. My shrunken arms looked like toothpicks against them, which was saying something, since they were children.

"What is it like, being here?" I asked softly, looking around at the lush green hills, the lake where the Isle of the Blessed lived, and the dome of a perfect summer sky.

"It is nice, Mama. There is no pain, but it is a sad place," Mermerus responded.

"Sad? Why, baby?"

He looked back at Pheres and then turned to me. "Only some members of a family may get in here. Some try for reincarnation and leave others behind, but mostly, people are apart from their loved ones and still retain their sense of self. Unlike in Asphodel, where you do not remember who you were."

I sighed. I had hoped that paradise would have grown a bit in the last few millennia.

"Is there anything you two need? I wish I could help, but even with my powers, I would be powerless to change this."

"For now, Mama," they replied in unison.

"Explain."

"We cannot, Mama, we only know that much. Something is changing in the world, a power shift of sorts. We think if you get your power back, that you may be a big part of it."

"I'm not sure I want them back, honestly." They stared at me, and I felt Vlad and Kide's eyes on the back of my head too.

"Why, Mama?" they asked in tandem.

I paused for a moment, thinking about everything I had accomplished, which had led me here.

"Because I am more without them. I am a better person. My powers were a burden. They made me Medea. Without them, though, I could just be a normal woman. One who is deeply, intrinsically bound to two men that I just can't give up. I would give up my powers, all of them, to stay by their side."

The smile that passed between Mermerus and Pheres was electric.

"That was the right answer."

My eyebrow raised in question before I felt the heat of the sun coursing through my body once more. As suddenly as they disappeared, my powers returned just as fast.

I cried out and stumbled back to my feet as Kide and Vlad rushed over. They stared at me and I held up my hands. While they remained small and frail from my lengthy ordeal in Tartarus, I saw ichor flowing beneath my skin again. The warm glow of the sun radiated around me, and with a quick gasp, I hugged them tightly.

"Also, Mama, we have two more bits of advice for you," They continued their speech in unison.

"What is it, my loves?" I knelt back down and took their hands in mine.

"First, be good and kind. Remember your lessons or your place with Aphrodite will switch, and you will remain in Tartarus all your days."

I nodded, understanding what they meant.

"And second, when you become a mother again, do not be afraid of the power of a name."

I cocked my head to the side, and they smiled. "Maybe not with the first one, but for your later children,"–I shuddered a little–"think on their names, for in their name will come their power."

I nodded again.

"We love you, Mama, and most importantly, we forgive you. We always have. But do you?" they asked me.

My answer was simple, quick, and honest.

"I do."

"Good. Now return to the surface world and go see your sister. She is worried sick about you," Mermerus said softly. "We will not be here, next time you look into the mirror, Pheres and I have decided to reincarnate. Maybe we will be lucky enough to have you as our Mama again."

I hugged both of them tightly and nodded.

"You should have done so long before now. But I am glad, and if we meet again under the sun, I will tell you I love you once more." I kissed their cheeks before their spirits dissipated back into the cauldron whence souls were born.

I stood up, turned to Kide and Vlad, and smiled sadly. "Let's go home."

It had been a couple of months since our return to the surface, and in that time, Kide and I had moved in with Vlad, but not in his Los Angeles mansion. He claimed that 'Hollywood was just too much for him' and he would return home to Romania.

This suited me just fine: city life – at least not American city life, with the pollution and the rudeness and the bland coffee – was not what I had in mind for my future.

We visited Chalkiope and the Ram first, letting her know that I was safe, and that my powers had returned. She cried far more than I had anticipated, but it was a good visit. Even with Aeëtes and Idyia there. Helios came to visit, and I pulled him aside to talk with him about Hyperion.

"I cannot say I am surprised, Medea," he replied. "My father is not one to share the spotlight. He is someone you will have to contend with, now that you are the official Titan of Light. The Colchian Throne is yours, when you wish to take it."

"Not yet. There is still much for me to do before I settle back down here."

He nodded knowingly and disappeared. In his place was Hekate, and the hug she gave me could have broken my back.

"Oh, my child!" she cried out, checking me over. "I can heal you, please let me help?"

"No, Hekate, I am fine. I want to heal the proper way, with time. So that my lessons do not dissipate with the wounds. All my scars too." As I spoke, every scar I had sustained over my long life appeared on my body. "I will keep them visible, as a reminder of my past, and guidance for my future."

My answer pleased her, and we continued to talk well into the night, before Kide and Vlad stole me away to return home.

As I healed from the incident in Tartarus – well, as my body returned to normal – I started looking at wedding details. There were no plans just yet, not with my impending meeting with Cernunnos looming closer. He had sent me time and date instructions, and, well, today was the day. Vlad, Kide, and I made our way into the dark Romanian forest, and awaited the Horned God.

"Medea!" a deep, commanding voice called out to me from the depths of the forest. Lord Cernunnos was beckoning me, and I had no choice but to obey.

I turned to look at my fiancés and smiled softly. "I promise I will return soon. Cernunnos said nothing about keeping me. Just breeding..." I couldn't even finish the sentence. The last conversation I had with the Horned God gave me the impression he would keep me busy for a while.

"Vlad, Kide, I love you both so very much. Remember, we have a wedding to plan. Did you think I was going to delay that?" They laughed but didn't speak. I felt a hook around my navel, pulling me into the forest. "I have to go. I love you." I kissed them both, giving all of my love to them, and then turned and walked into the dark forest, into the home of the Horned God.

"Ah, Medea, look at you. Fully reinstated as your Titan self, and the Titan of Light to boot." Cernunnos sat on a tree stump, one leg crossed over the other, naked as a newborn babe. I nearly crumpled from the pheromones he emitted.

"You don't need to entice me, Lord Cernunnos," I smiled softly as I approached, my clothing disappearing in a blaze of flame. "I come here of my own free will, to repay my end of our bargain." The smile that lit upon the old god's face almost had me withering with desire.

Cernunnos crooked his finger at me, and I took another step towards him.

"Mmm, Medea," he crooned, inhaling deeply, "I can smell your potency from here. One night is all it will take, I think. The rest will be for fun. You will not want to leave."

"The rest?" I shivered. He had reigned in his pheromones, yet I still felt their power, still felt his essence washing over me.

The Horned God stood and took the last step between us before hooking a finger under my chin, lifting my gaze to meet his.

"Oh yes. One week, Medea. I was not sure how long it would take, but your body has been waiting for this, for me... for them... for eons. You are the matriarch of the new era, Medea, your dynastic line begins tonight, your crown prince will be *my* son." Cernunnos lifted me, his fingers wrapped around my back, brushing the scars from my mortal life.

"Do not fret, child, your men will have their heirs, but mine, he will be the most powerful of them all. Imagine, the sea, the sun, the forests and beasts, all under the domain of one god." He bristled with anticipation as my legs wrapped around his waist, drawing him in close.

"I don't understand. No one mentioned this to me when I was in Tartarus." My mind was hazy. Lust coursed through every fiber of my being.

Cernunnos brought his lips down on mine and I moaned deeply, a tidal wave of desire flooding through my body. When he spoke next, it was without words; I felt him in my soul.

"Nor will you remember these words when you leave my realm. But I promise you, Medea, your destiny is far from over. You may be of the old pantheon, but you are the youngest of them. When they fade, when *we* fade, and I promise Medea—we are fading—you and your children will usher in a new golden age. One where magic and gods, where religion and belief are one. Science is catching up. It will be up to you and your line to show them the rest of the way."

I shuddered. A vision of the peace and prosperity Cernunnos had described flitted across my mind, and I couldn't help but be amazed. I felt his giant cock resting right at my slit, teasing the opening to my core, and I rocked my hips gently but insistently against him.

"Well then, shall we greet the new era, my Lord?"

With one swift movement, the Lord of the Hunt, the Horned God, the King of Beasts and Wild Spaces thrust up into me and I understood in a heartbeat what he had been saying. He was fertility incarnate. There was no possible way it would take him more than one night to impregnate me. By morning I would be with child. And he was right. I wanted to stay the rest of the week. I wanted to claim this god for whatever time I had with him, to use this glorious cock for my own pleasure.

"Oh Medea, you may use me as you see fit, but if anyone is claiming anything, it will be *I* claiming *you*." Cernunnos' deep voice echoed in my soul once more before we devolved into the frenetic dance we were creating.

By morning, as I lay in the arms of Cernunnos, Lord and lover, I heard the soft whisper of a voice in my ear. My boys were welcoming their baby brother into our hearts. "Kaden," I whispered softly, a single tear falling down my cheek onto Cernunnos' chest.

I felt him rumble beneath me and placed his hand over my stomach. Without cracking open an eye, the Lord of the Forest kissed me deeply, lovingly, as Vlad or Kide would have, and smiled. "Kaden is a beautiful name. Welcome to the world, my son. Your mother and I are waiting for you."

THE END

Associated Short Stories

A Fate Sealed

Chalkiope and I always played at the wrought iron gates that separated Colchis from the garden of the dragon. Chal liked playing with her older sister and me, well... I could sense the magic of the Golden Fleece for miles. It was intoxicating. I already had a penchant for mixing herbs and tonics, and when I found one that put my perfect sister to sleep, I upped the dosage. I wanted to try it out on the Colchian dragon. That beast never slept, and I needed to see the Golden Fleece.

"Medea, I do not think this is a good idea," Chalkiope whimpered as we opened the gate.

I looked at my younger sister and smiled.

"Then go back, this is something I need to do. I need to prove myself to Kirke somehow." Chalkiope understood how much learning magic from our aunt meant to me, and she nodded.

"Ok, so what do we do then?" She asked, her voice still nervous, but I could hear the confidence in it, and that touched me. I pulled out a large stone and smiled darkly. It was the first time I had smiled like that, but it would not be the last, not by a long shot.

"We are going to lure him to us... using this. The dragon, while protective, is curious. He does not roast trespassers immediately. We will throw the boulder somewhere in the opposite direction, and then I will run in front and throw the sachet in his face. I want you to stay as far away as you can, Chal, please." She nodded and sighed. "If it works, I will wave you over, if not well... I love you, and tell mater and pater that I loved them too." That was not entirely the truth, but she was too young to appreciate why I disliked my parents.

Chalkiope gripped my hand and smiled weakly. I ran in, hurling the stone as far away from me as I could. The dragon went for the stone, and I made a dash for his muzzle. I needed to get as close as possible for this to work.

When the beast focused on the stone, I approached as close as I dared and then hurled the sachet, yelling at him as I did. "Open up, you great beast!" The dragon roared and swallowed the sachet whole.

The poultice did not seem to be working so I turned and hauled ass back to the gate, hoping to escape his fiery wrath. But it never came. I looked back and saw a dazed look on the dragon's face, then he went slack, fell off the tree and began snoring. I looked at Chalkiope and waved her on. We went over to the Colchian dragon, the beast that never slept, and I placed a gentle hand on his muzzle. "Sleep well my friend, you have earned it." I did not know how long the poultice would last, so my sister and I made our way to the tree, where the Golden Fleece rested. Instinct took over, and I touched it gently.

"Medea, what are you doing?" Chalkiope whispered angrily.

I just shut my eyes and felt its power flow through me. So much was shown to me then, and I realised my destiny would be far greater than being married off to some random prince and ruling Colchis under him. But first, I would need to prove to Kirke that I deserved to learn from her and Hekate.

While Chalkiope was glancing back at the dragon, I stole a strand of the fleece and tucked it into my chiton.

"Can we go now?" Chal hissed at me and I smiled.

"Yes, we can go. We will retreat to the gates, I want to know just how long this will last." I whispered as we jogged back to the gates and closed them.

"Remember, we cannot tell anyone else about this, got it?" Chalkiope nodded quickly and ran off, back to the palace. I had a feeling she would never return with me here.

As for me, I waited to see how long the sleep would last so that I could adjust the poultice. I would stand guard over the dragon when he was unable to. This small act, this unknown gesture, sparked a bond between myself and the Colchian dragon that lasted the rest of our lives. I just did not know how quickly the man, not just the beast, would come into play.

"Medea!" My great-grandfather's voice cut through the fog of my pain as another reminder of his strength sliced across my face. The blade he was using burned hot as the sun, cauterising the wound instantly. I rubbed my face and stared up at Hyperion, Lord of the East, as he towered over me.

"How will you ever learn to wield my power if you do not concentrate?" His tone sent another lash of power my way and I dodged it, jumping into the air and arching backwards. I landed on my feet gracefully, immediately thankful for my dance lessons.

"I am only thirteen, Lord Hyperion, I have barely begun to harness your power, let alone control it!" My retort fell on deaf ears as another blade of sun fire arced my way and I spun fluidly out of danger and into the strong arms of a man.

My eyes lifted to his, shining like dark obsidian orbs down at me, and there was a hint of a smirk in his gaze.

"Who are you?" Hyperion demanded. The man held my gaze, and I was utterly spellbound by his presence. There was a faint familiarity to it, but I could not place from where.

"I am named Kidemonos," he replied. *Kidemonos*, the word meant "protector", or "guardian", but who or what was he guarding?

"Umm, excuse me?" I piped up and Kidemonos looked back at me. "Would you mind letting me go?"

His arms dropped from around my back and I immediately felt a rush of cool air separate us when he stepped back.

"My apologies, my princess, I did not mean to offend." Kidemonos dropped into a deep respectful bow, and I felt heat rush to my cheeks. I turned away quickly and shook my head.

"You did not offend; I am just not used to the arms of a man." Now, why in Hades did I say that?

A dark growl emanated from Kidemonos, and I shook once more, the beginnings of impure thoughts tied to that growl flitted across my mind.

"Nor should you be," he replied before Hyperion coughed rather rudely.

"As touching as this is, you have yet to explain who you are and why you are here." He demanded. Even though this was the house of Aeëtes my father and King of Colchis, whenever Hyperion or Helios, Aeëtes' father, were around, the throne and realm was theirs. This was the East, their domain reigned supreme.

"As I said, great Hyperion," Kidemonos flourished a bow to my great-grandfather, "my name is Kidemonos. I am the guardian of the Golden Fleece, and I am here to bond with your great-granddaughter and the future Queen of Colchis."

Our jaws hit the floor as Hyperion and I stared at the stranger, or maybe that was my ass as I sat down with a thud.

"You cannot, she has only just come of age, her father and I have not yet discussed marriage opportunities for her yet. But I can promise you this, Medea will never be Queen of Colchis." Hyperion spat, beads of hardened fire rained like droplets down onto the marble floor.

Kidemonos simply smiled. "I do not wish to wed her," I could almost hear an unspoken *yet* in the sentence, but I knew that was not the case, "simply merge our powers and bodies into one, separate yet together. We will both be the guardians of the Fleece, Colchis will prosper and you will gain a formidable new ally in your everlasting feud with the gods."

As Kidemonos spoke, I could see the wheels turning in Hyperion's mind. The mention of power nearly had him salivating. "She would be powerful enough to take on a few of them, would she not? Perhaps some of the lesser gods, Dionysos or Zagreus, perhaps, to test her abilities, and yours."

"Oh, not yet sir, but eventually yes. I would love for us both to be strong enough to eventually stand toe to toe with you." Kidemonos replied confidently. "That would be the only way to assure you that Colchis and the East are in the best hands. But she will need one more thing."

Hyperion laughed haughtily and sat down, looking Kidemonos level in the eye. "And what is that, little dragonling?"

I heard the insult, even if I did not truly understand what it meant. There was a hiss behind me, and sulphur flooded the room.

"She is to train with her aunt and Hekate. She needs her magic, as much as she needs your power. Perhaps even more." Kidemonos demanded.

Hyperion appeared to contemplate the offer, but he nodded after a moment. "Agreed." With that he disappeared in a flash of blinding light, and I scrambled back up to my feet.

"You are the dragon?" I asked softly, looking up at Kidemonos once more.

"I am, that sleeping draught you made me was amazing. Thank you."

He took my right hand, kissed the top and bowed gracefully. "I meant what I said princess, I will help make you powerful enough to take on Hyperion. To take down Hyperion."

I did not miss the hint in his voice, but then Chalkiope burst in crying that Absyrtus was teasing her again. When I turned to explain to Kidemonos what was going on, I found that he had disappeared.

Dust Up in Adrano

After five hundred years, Sicily bored me. I knew I needed a change, and Kidemonos was so wrapped up in his work with Hephaestus that when I told him I was heading off-island to visit Milan, he merely nodded. Milan was one of my favourite cities in the world, and I took every opportunity I had to visit her vibrant streets. Reconnecting with the Medici family would be fun as well.

I had barely reached the outskirts of my beloved city when Kidemonos' voice sounded in my head.

Medea! Get back to Sicily now!

I stopped, rolled my eyes, and turned back. I could have translocated myself here originally, but I liked the walk, even if it took me a few months to get here. I was in no rush, and I certainly was not in any hurry to return to Adrano.

Why, Kidemonos, have you finished your apprenticeship?

I will be honest here: I was a little jealous. I loved my dragon, my soul-bonded partner. We had been together for millennia, but he could have a life. If we separated, he could be his own man. There were things, constraints put on my activities because of my past. A stabbing pain erupted in my heart as I recalled the beautiful faces of my sons, Mermerus and Pheres, as the hemlock took them in their sleep, never to awaken.

No, you ingrate! Ok, he was cross with me. He had never called me such names before. *Adrano has become a hotbed for vampiric activity in the months since your departure. Even my master has made note of it.*

Now that made me pause. If Hephaestus noticed humans were dying at an alarming rate, as they tend to do when fed on by the creatures of the night, there must be a problem indeed.

And what does this have to do with me? I replied sarcastically.

You are the only one who has been holding them back. They feared coming forward, Medea! I winced at the whip in his voice.

I am only one woman, Kidemonos.

You are the most feared sorceress in the world, Medea. People would rather deal with Baba Yaga than with you.

Fine, fine, I will return. I did not want to, not when I was so close to Milan. *But then I am leaving again, Kidemonos. I will not be sequestered in that tiny backwater town for another five hundred years.*

As you wish Medea, but please, hurry. There may be no humans left when you return.

I sighed. Kidemonos had a point. I am sure the Erinyes would love to know how I turned my back on a town and let them be slaughtered by a bunch of disgusting vampires. The sun was setting on Milan, and I heard the jubilant peal of the bells even from out here on the side of the road. A shriek escaped my lips. Freedom was so close. I could just ignore Kidemonos... but then my boys' faces appeared in my mind's eye, standing before me as if they were physical, and I nodded. I knew the portent. My path lay back in Adrano, not in Milan.

The translocation brought me to the center of town. The piazza was empty, which was odd. Adrano normally had a bustling evening life, and that was when I picked up the first hints of blood in the air. That coppery taste was unique. A touch of iron in it helped me identify the blood as human.

The sky was not yet dark enough for the vampires to come out and play, so I began searching for survivors, clues, anything to help focus me on who created this coven, and why they laid siege to this town. I did not want to believe Kidemonos when he said it was because I had left.

A young girl, maybe 6 or 7 years of age, sobbed quietly in a house nearby. I homed in on the location and sent myself there immediately, hoping she was not being attacked then. Dark blue eyes gazed up at me under a mop of curly black hair and for a moment I thought I was looking at my sister, Chalkiope. Blue was a rare colour here in the Mediterranean, so every time I saw the startling colour, it reminded me of my sister.

"Hello little one, where are your mother and father?" I spoke calmly, kneeling down so that I could look her in the eyes. I may not have been the world's greatest mother, but I knew how to deal with children. The little girl jumped into my arms and buried her face in my neck. I cradled the poor child, knowing instantly what happened.

"Dead, both of them. Papa two nights ago, mama last night. I do not want to get eaten!" She squealed and started bawling.

"Shush baby, Auntie is here to help. I will take care of the monsters and find you a new home to live in." I replied, stroking the hair of the little girl and carrying her to the small house I had been using these last few centuries to tuck her into bed. "Sleep, little one, no one will hunt you tonight." I placed my hand on her forehead and laid a small protection spell over her before helping her to sleep. I waited to hear the little girl's soft snores before I left.

The air had cooled off while I was tending to the child, and I looked up at the black sky. Everything was still and quiet. I sealed up the wards on my house and made my way back to the piazza after cutting open my palm. Little drops of blood trailed behind me. I knew what would draw them in, and divine blood always did the trick.

Like sharks homing in on the weakened fish, I felt the presence of my predators surrounding me. One by one, I saw crimson-soaked eyes glaring at me from the shadows.

"Come out, little demons," I called out. They responded with a collective hiss of annoyance. It only made me laugh. "I am just a woman, alone, in the middle of the night. Why do you hesitate?"

A feral growl sounded behind me and I spun around to see the first vampire attack just in time to dodge it, avoiding his fangs. The male reached out with his claws and grabbed my arm. It almost hurt. I shook the vampire off after sending a burst of fire down my arm and to his hand. He reeled back, screaming, and cursed me. I simply smiled at him.

"You do not know who you are dealing with, fire witch," he growled again, pulling back his charred hand. "We are the children of Ambrose."

Shit. Of all the vampire covens I had to cross, I found one of his. Ambrose was the oldest vampire I knew of, if not the original. We had stayed away from each other our entire lives, nearly three-thousand years of them, and now it appeared we were coming to a head.

"Well, I do not fear Ambrose, but you all should fear me. It is *you* who do not know who you are dealing with." I held my right hand out, palm up, as a whip of fire, burning bright orange, formed in it. The piazza glowed as if daylight had come early and I watched the vampires shrink back.

"Who is first?" I dropped my hand so that it was hanging beside me and smirked at the various vampires around me. Foolish babies, thinking it was simply fire.

They leapt individually, and I lashed out expertly, cracking the whip around throats and through chests. I grabbed arms and threw a disintegrating vampire into a small group, who were unsure of whether or not to attack. They were brave, I will give them that.

Tactics changed, and they began attacking in pairs, some hanging back and waiting for an opening, but never seeing one. I created a second whip in my left hand and used them in tandem. This made them pause.

"Who are you who wields such devastating fire?" One female asked. I sneered at her, cracked the whip around her throat and pulled, decapitating her effortlessly.

"Medea," I replied, my voice a deadly whisper. A ripple passed through the remaining vampires. I felt one or two escape, but before the rest of them fled my wrath, I raised my hands and lit up the piazza with my fire. The sun rose early in Adrano that night, and none of the remaining vampires survived. I felt each disintegration. Every cry split my ears open. I shook with the effort it took to consume them, but in the end, I knew it had to be done. Whatever populace was left here needed to be protected.

When I felt the last vampire fade in the torrent of my flames, I lowered my hands, snuffing the fire. I leaned back against the wall, wheezing, and sent a quick thought up to Kidemonos.

It is done. Only a couple survived. I am done for the night.

I was sure he could hear the wheezing in my thoughts, and I closed my eyes for a moment. That was when I felt it. Cold air, a dark presence nearby that had not been there a moment ago. I stood up and strode back over to the center of the piazza and waited for him. I knew who it was, who it had to be. The babies ran back to Daddy.

"Ambrose, it has been a long time coming," I commented as the spectral figure appeared before me.

"Who do you think you are, little witch?" His voice boomed, reverberating through my soul. He was as ancient as I was, but Ambrose looked his age.

I squared my shoulders and looked up into his dark eyes, unafraid. "Medea." My voice was calm, solid in my confidence.

I watched as the weary-looking vampire's face twisted in shock, and then he laughed. "You died in Athens after betraying everyone you loved." My fingers lit with bright orange fire, matching my rage, and denying my exhaustion, and I smiled darkly as Ambrose recoiled. "You should not exist."

"No, you are correct. I should not. Yet, here I am, defending the remaining innocents of this town." I felt like I could redeem some small part of my wicked soul if I took down this abomination.

"There is no one to come to your rescue, no one who will stand beside you. This town is mine." I snorted as his assertion fell on deaf ears. Kide roared above me, a black outline against a blacker sky. The Colchian Dragon landed beside me, and my heart soared for all of five seconds before I realized what this meant. Kide had given up his apprenticeship with Hephaestus.

Then, to my shock, the lame god, as Vulcan, burst forth in a pillar of flame. The heat that radiated off him was immense, and if I had been anyone else, I would have died from it. "My lord Vulcan," I said with a bow, showing both my respect and my gratitude. He grunted at me, and I knew I upset him. I had not expected either of them to show. I planned on taking out Ambrose alone.

I flinched and turned back to Ambrose and saw the shock in his eyes. "So, you have friends?"

I shook my head and sighed. "It is called a family, Ambrose. I am sorry I had to end yours, but they were making themselves known to the mortals. You cannot just wipe out a town for food. Or for fun." He just stared at me. "Leave, Ambrose; I do not wish for a fight, even if the dragon and Vulcan had not arrived. I would have won."

Ambrose snarled at me, fangs and claws extended. "I have a family too, the most powerful child I have created yet." I shivered at the thought of just what kind of vampire this would be and prepared to do what was necessary to end him. "We are not done, Medea. You and I will meet again, and you will not have your *family* with you." He burst into a mass of bats and took off into the night. I turned and looked at Kide, the sadness creeping into his eyes now that the threat was gone. I blew it.

Hephaestus took off, trudging back up the mountain the old-fashioned way, while Kidemonos and I ambled along behind him. Our heads hung low in shame, mine lower than his. I had not been in any real danger. Vampires posed no threat to me. So why did he break his oath and leave the service of Hephaestus? It was a question I would not get the answer to until centuries later, when I faced off with Ambrose next.

A Vampire and A Sorceress

Medea, this is a bad idea. Kide's voice rang in my head. He did not normally intrude on my thoughts, but it had been a century or two since my ordeal with Ambrose. I recently took a contract to exterminate a powerful vampire as I could not dislodge the idea of ridding the world of the threat of Ambrose's creation. I spent those years researching him, and his clan. I looked everywhere for clues as to who this mystery child of his was, but I drew a blank.

I know, Kide, I know. But what else can I do? This guy apparently impales his victims and leaves them on his doorstep. We cannot let this continue! I was stern, knowing my dragon agreed with me, he just hated letting me go into danger. We were down in the Vatican archives, not that they knew we were there, but the wealth of information here always astounded me.

What was the name again Medea? Kide asked.

"Vlad Drăculea," I whispered softly. The candles snuffed out as I said his name. Any mortal would have taken that as an indication of the power of his name, but I was not any mortal.

And you are sure the Holy Roman Pope wants us to remove him? Kide inquired.

We had gone over this a dozen or so times since the letter came to us in Turkey. Though, how they knew where to send it and who to address it to currently escaped me.

Yes, I am as shocked as you are, Kide, but all we can do for now is head over to Transylvania and do what we can. I feel... wrong... taking a contract from the Church. I shivered slightly and relit the candles before getting up. Closing the book we were reading sent waves of dust through the room and I heard a cough echo around the corner.

"Who is there? Answer quickly, or die." Yes, I was probably threatening a priest, or a cardinal, but I did not care. What power did they have over me?

"I am but a simple monk, who cares for these tomes," a terrified voice sounded up from the floor. The young man scurried out from behind a bookshelf and stood up. The poor thing was shaking. He must be freezing in that woolen smock.

"A simple man who loves his work, I can tell." I smiled easily, even though my skin was crawling. The Church and I had a very rocky relationship, and I did not wish to further frighten this man.

"I do, but is it true? Are you going after the Impaler?" I nodded simply. "Then you must be Medea!" He squeaked and cowered away from me.

I sighed and nodded again before heading to the door.

"You have nothing to fear, little man, but who better to send after a monster, than a monster?" I turned and smiled back at him before vanishing through the open door.

Winter was approaching, and I knew I did not want to be stuck in the mountains in a blizzard. Kide and I had translocated as close to Transylvania territory as I felt comfortable entering without announcing myself. Maybe he knew we were coming. I did not know, but it would not do for me to be unprepared here.

"Gods," I shivered, "it is cold here."

I ran my hands over my body and formed a thick fur coat over me.

Really Medea? You could have just warmed yourself up the way you normally do. Kide snorted.

And inform anyone that I meet that I am supernatural? Magic is seriously mistrusted here; I need to be careful. I replied in kind. Witch-hunters loved these dark foreboding mountains, and so did many of my sisters. It is why the Black Forest in Germany had so many of us. Even I had a home there, one I would be glad to return to once this monster was dealt with. *Let us head into town, see what information we can gather. I would rather not just march up to his castle. Sometimes stealth is the better option.*

I suppose so, Kide agreed. *I could always fly overhead and scout the area out, maybe burn a few castles down, just to be safe.*

No. I cannot even begin to fathom the reaction people would have seeing a dragon in the vicinity, even one as glorious as you, my friend. Did you forget? They called his father the Dragon. His house is the Dragon. Do you wish to reinforce that belief among the villagers?

I felt Kide still in my mind before the mental image of him shaking his head. *No, that would cause a panic.*

Soon enough, my friend, we will fly together, to raze and hunt. But for now...

...you need to work. He replied softly.

It took us a week to descend into Transylvania and find a village with a decent inn. I only had a few standards when it came to rooms, cleanliness topped that list. Kide was less picky, but since we were using my body, it was ultimately my decision. When we flew as a dragon, the den's were his pick.

"The Dragon's Keep" was poetically named and it welcomed me with a crackling fire, and the scent of roasting meat. A handsome young man was behind the bar, and I walked over slowly.

"Good evening," he smiled up at me, a flash of white between pale lips and I smiled cordially back. He smelled off, and I could not quite place why.

"Good evening, I would like a room please, for the foreseeable future." He looked down at me. The barkeep easily had a head of height above me and nodded.

"For one or two people?" He asked, grabbing a book and quill.

"One." His head snapped up from his scribbling and I realized my mistake. Kide and I should have split off. We normally did when we had to travel like this. Women were not supposed to be alone, especially in these smaller provinces. "I am a widower, and I plan to write about the world my late husband always wanted to see."

Really Medea? Kide chortled to me. *A widower?*

Well, I am! I replied, no outward expression showing on my face. "Do you have something free, Sir...?"

"Tepes, and yes, I do." He replied calmly. My mouth fell open and black eyes stared at me.

"My apologies. Any relation to *the* Vlad Tepes?" He nodded, looking a little uncomfortable. "My apologies again, Sir Tepes, I mean no disrespect. Even as far away as Rome, people have heard of him."

"Oh yes, I know they have. Every season they send a new young vampire hunter to test their skills against him. None ever returned."

I shuddered appropriately, though unafraid. It surprised me that the Church would send new hunters against him, instead of against some of the other threats and then off to the Impaler.

"I am Medeline," I replied, holding my hand out. He took it cautiously, and the instant we touched I knew why. He was a vampire. Kide recoiled in my mind, but I knew I had to remain calm.

"It is a pleasure, Medeline. Shall I show you to your room?" He asked and slid out from the bar. He was dressed as a bartender should be, plain linen shirt and brown trousers with an apron around his waist, but the way he stood was different. His shoulders were straight, unhunched from years of tending a bar. He was taller than I thought too. It was more than confidence, more than knowing you were the owner of some bar. The air around this man bristled with unbridled power and I shivered as I took his arm.

"Please, that would be most gracious." I could not help but wonder just what he was capable of, both in scope of strength, and as a potential lover.

We walked together slowly through the tavern and up the stairs to the third floor. There was only one room at the top of the stairs, and it was elegantly decorated. My eyes sparkled when I walked in.

"Occasionally the Voivode will entertain guests in the village, and this room offers them a place to retire without having to travel all the way back to the castle."

He stepped into the room and latched the door, as Kide began shouting warnings in my head that I did not need.

"I am sure flying all the way back there with brides or food would be quite inconvenient, would it not be, Vlad?" I asked, turning to him, and smiling brightly.

"You are a quick little hunter, but unfortunately tonight is your last night in this fair land." He moved incredibly fast and if I had been anyone else, I would never have seen him.

I took a step into his presence the moment he stopped and watched as his eyes flashed crimson.

"How did you do that?" he demanded.

"You are not the only special one here, little vampire. I was, however, sent to kill you, so I do apologize. You are a wonderful host." A stake appeared in my hand and Vlad cowered back.

"What are you?" He demanded.

"A witch. The name is Medea," I stated softly before appearing in front of him. "You may as well die with the truth, instead of believing a lie." Snake-tight arms wrapped around my body and pulled me up against him.

"Let me go," I squirmed. I was hesitant to use my fire here, the tavern and village were built from sturdy timber for sure, but it would still burn.

"No," he growled, and I whimpered. I what? His lips crashed down on mine and for a moment I forgot why I was here, what I was hired to do. I forgot about Kide, about my past, about anything else except the feeling of his lips on mine.

After a breathless moment, when Vlad finally pulled his lips back and I stared up at him, a dark smile crept over his face.

"I will enjoy you hunting me, Medea, the great Sorceress of Colchis." His voice was a whisper before he disappeared into the night sky.

Pronunciation Guide

- **Absyrtus:** *Ancient Greek: Ἄψυρτος, Apsurtus*

- **Acheron:** *Ancient Greek: Ἀχέρων, Acheron*

- **Aea:** *Ancient Greek: Αἶα, A-ee-a*

- **Aeëtes:** *Ancient Greek: Αἰήτης, Aiếtēs*

- **Aegeus:** *Ancient Greek: Αἰγεύς, Aigeús*

- **Aetna:** *Ancient Greek: Αἴτνη Aĭtnē*

- **Asklepius:** *Ancient Greek: Ἀσκληπιός Asklēpiós*

- **Cernunnos:** *Kern-ū-nos*

- **Chalkiope:** *Ancient Greek: Χαλκιόπη, Khalkiópē*

- **Charon:** *Ancient Greek: Χάρων, Kharon*

- **Charybdis:** *Ancient Greek: Χάρυβδις, kʰárybdis, Kharubdis*

- **Colchis:** *Ancient Greek: Κολχίς, Kolkis*

- **Elysian:** *Ancient Greek: Ἡλύσιον, Ēlýsion*

- **Hekate:** *Ancient Greek: Ἑκάτη, Hekátē*

- **Helios:** *Ancient Greek: Ἥλιος, Helios*

- **Hephaestus:** *Ancient Greek: Ἥφαιστος, Hḗphaistos*

- **Hyperion:** *Ancient Greek: Ὑπερίων. Huperion*

- **Idyia:** *Ancient Greek: Ἰδυῖα, Idyîa*

- **Kidemonos:** *Kee-day-mo-nos;* **Kide:** *Kee-day*

- **Kirke:** *Ancient Greek: Κίρκη, kírkε*

- **Medea:** *Ancient Greek: Μήδεια, Mēdeia*

- **Medeius:** *Ancient Greek: Μηδείας or Μήδειος, Medeias/Medeios*

- **Mermerus:** *Ancient Greek: Μέρμερος, Mérmeros, Mermerus*

- **Pasiphaë:** *Ancient Greek: Πασιφάη Pasipháē*

- **Perseis:** *Ancient Greek: Περσηίς, Persēís*

- **Pheres:** *Ancient Greek: Φέρης, Phéres, Féris, Pheres*

- **Xiphos:** *Ancient Greek: ξίφος, ksíphos, ksi-phōs*

Important Locations

In order of appearance in the book:

- Eastsound, Orcas Island Washington, USA (Where Medea and Kide live)

- Transylvania, Romania (Originally to find Vlad)

- Los Angeles, California, USA (Where Vlad lives)

- Adrano, Sicily, Italy (Hephaestus)

- Lagina, Turkey (Hekate)

- Athens, Attica, Greece (Jason)

- Kutaisi, Aea, Georgia (Aeëtes and Idyia)

- Parga, Ephesus, Greece (Entrance to the Underworld)

- The Underworld:

  - Acheron River

  ○

Palace of Hades (Hyperion)

- ○ Fields of Asphodel (Asklepius and Thanatos)

- ○ Tartarus (Alekto, Medea's punishment)

- ○ Elysian Fields (Mermerus and Pheres)

- Transylvania, Romania (Where the trio end up settling down, Cernunnos)

Use the QR code to listen to my *Remaking the Sorceress* writing playlist.